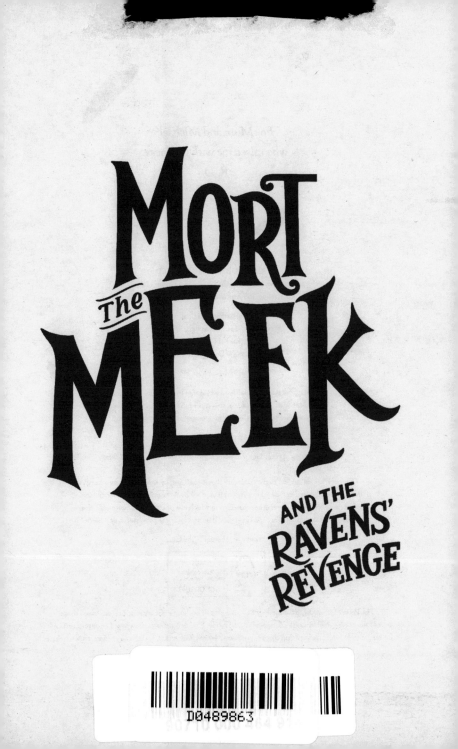

MORT _The_ MEEK

AND THE RAVENS' REVENGE

D0489863

For Mum and Michael,
who raised me with kindness.
R. D.

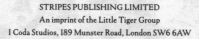

STRIPES PUBLISHING LIMITED
An imprint of the Little Tiger Group
1 Coda Studios, 189 Munster Road, London SW6 6AW

A paperback original
First published in Great Britain in 2021
Text © Rachel Delahaye, 2021
Illustrations © George Ermos, 2021

ISBN: 978-1-78895-314-6

The right of Rachel Delahaye and George Ermos to be identified
as the author and illustrator of this work has been asserted by them
in accordance with the Copyright, Designs and Patents Act, 1988.

All rights reserved.

A CIP catalogue record for this book is available from the British Library.

This book is sold subject to the condition that it shall not, by way of trade or otherwise,
be lent, resold, hired out, or otherwise circulated without the publisher's prior consent in
any form of binding or cover other than that in which it is published and without a similar
condition including this condition being imposed upon the subsequent purchaser.

Printed and bound in the UK.

MIX
Paper from
responsible sources
FSC® C020471

The Forest Stewardship Council® (FSC®) is a global, not-for-profit organization dedicated to the
promotion of responsible forest management worldwide. FSC defines standards based on agreed principles
for responsible forest stewardship that are supported by environmental, social, and economic stakeholders.
To learn more, visit www.fsc.org

2 4 6 8 10 9 7 5 3 1

MORT THE MEEK

AND THE RAVENS' REVENGE

RACHEL DELAHAYE
ILLUSTRATED BY GEORGE ERMOS

LITTLE TIGER
LONDON

**LONDON BOROUGH OF
RICHMOND UPON THAMES**

90710 000 464 914

Askews & Holts	17-Mar-2021
JF	
RTR	

DISCARDED FROM

RICHMOND UPON THAMES

LIBRARY SERVICE

CHAPTER ONE
THE RAVENS
OF BRUTALIA

"Ah, Brutalia..."

"Place of peace!"

"Shores of delight!"

"Land of loveliness!"

"Aaaaah-ha-ha-ha-ha-ha!"

Anyone who tells you that Brutalia was a peaceful and lovely place with delightful shores is either a pants-on-fire liar or a raven with a terrible sense of humour. Because the truth was this: surrounded by a dark grey sea that spat like a badly behaved child, Brutalia was an island of terrifying ugliness.

To make things worse, it was ruled by a Queen and King who were not only terrifyingly ugly, but also BRUTAL.

The Queen and King made laws against everything beautiful – like celebrating a birthday, or playing in the sun, or singing *fa-la-la-la-laaaa* for the fun of it. And there were always punishments for breaking these laws. Some punishments stung, like nose-twisting and wasp baths. Other punishments – like being forced to wear spiky underwear – hurt a lot. Some of them were *really* painful (if you've ever had a toe or finger chopped off, you'll know what I mean).

And then there was the ultimate punishment – death. That was the Queen's favourite. She loved it so much, she decided to make it Brutalia's motto:

LIVE OR DIE

It wasn't the most inspirational motto of all time. But if you ever said that aloud you'd be breaking the law and would probably **DIE**.

Most people tried not to **DIE**. And, so long as they didn't get up the Queen and King's noses, many of them actually managed to **LIVE** and carry on with thumping their neighbours for no good reason and eating worms for tea. Hunger was everywhere and violence was rife.

From the day they were born, the people of Brutalia knew only misery. There were regular beatings and measly food rations, making everyone extremely grouchy. And, while the Queen and King lived in a grand palace, everyone else struggled in total poverty in the shadow of the island's two badly built towers, which stuck out of the Salty Sea like a giant danger sign in the mist. A bit like this:

Visitors were **NOT** welcome. (It even said **Not Welcome** on its sign.)

Woe betide any passing sailor who ignored these words or succumbed to the friendly cheer of "Ahoy! Ahoy!" carried to them on the wind. Because an "Ahoy! Ahoy!" from that island was not friendly. Not one little bit.

It was the call of Brutalia's ravens, who had cunningly adapted their cry to lure sailors into the craggy bays of Brutalia where they would meet their fate on the rocks. During the day, the ravens circled Brutalia, searching the ragged shoreline for distressed sailors. Or at least some body parts of distressed sailors. A plump eyeball was always nice.

Beware the ravens of Brutalia! said no one. Because no one ever survived to pass on the message.

On this particular day, the ravens were circling and dreaming of brains. Or, more specifically, parts of the brain that were especially flavoursome.

"Oi," said one raven. "Wouldn't you just die for an amygdala?"

"I like the hippocampus," said another.

"What about the thalamus?" said a third raven, flapping alongside. "Got a lovely nutty flavour."

"Frontal lobe for me," added another.

"Yeah, frontal lobe..." one said dreamily. "Yum."

But it was wishful thinking. There were no brains or kidneys or livers for them today. Not even a whiff of sailor... In fact, there hadn't been a whiff of anything meaty for weeks.

Once upon a time, gory bits would bob to the surface like ping-pong balls in a bathtub, but the supply had mysteriously stopped. The ravens were lucky to suck on a toenail clipping brought to them on the tide. It's hard not to feel sorry for the hungry birds, but you mustn't. If they spot weakness, they'll descend on you like babies on a banana...

Desperate for food, the ravens had taken to hanging round Brutalia's houses, hoping for scraps. But the people were also starving, so there were never any leftovers. And, even if there had been, throwing out scraps was a crime punishable by death.

This sets the scene nicely, don't you think?

The Queen and King were horrible.

The people were violent.

And the ravens were ravenous.

CHAPTER TWO
RAVEN PIE

"Would it hurt to try fruit?"

"It would hurt our image as the evil,
meat-ripping ravens of Brutalia.
THE EVIL, APPLE-CRUNCHING BIRDS
doesn't have quite the same ring."

It was the trial of Weed Millet, the baker's son, and the people of Brutalia were gathered in the square to witness it. When they were about to be horrible to someone, the Queen and King made everyone watch. It was to keep the people on their toes. (Those whose toes hadn't been cut off, which was last month's *non-death punishment of choice*.)

Weed was on his knees at the feet of the royal couple. He was only twelve but his hard life made him look thirteen and a half.

As he was still a child, and therefore not old enough to be given a death sentence, Weed was hoping his punishment would be no harsher than a spell of poo-collecting. At worst it would be the removal of his earlobes (this month's *non-death punishment of choice* and not so bad, unless you liked wearing earrings).

Weed widened his beautiful chocolatey eyes at the royals, hoping they would see his innocence and think twice about doing something nasty. But the Queen's face was pinched, and the King's potato face gave nothing away – probably because it was bloated from a life of fatty foods and sluggishness. Too lazy to talk, he hardly ever said a word. The Queen, however, was very vocal. And she was also in a **terrible mood** (the King had spent the morning trying to kiss her – utterly revolting).

"If you were a child," she said, "I might consider making my punishment *not* death."

"I am a child," Weed said. "I'm only twelve. You can ask the scribe."

Unfortunately, at that very moment, Scribe Pockle (Keeper of Birth Certificates and Legal Documents) was in prison (and missing one finger) for spilling ink on the Queen's carpet.

"Poppycock! I don't need Scribe Pockle to tell me. You look thirteen and a half, and not a day younger. Under Brutalia's laws, that makes you a grown man. That is my final word." (It clearly wasn't going to be her final word – she never stopped talking.)

Weed opened his mouth to protest.

"Someone stop this fool from whimpering!" the Queen snapped. **"NOW!"**

A guard stepped forward and growled menacingly at Weed, the baker's son, making him whimper.

"He's still making noises!"

"Sorry, Your Majesty," the guard said, bowing frantically to show how sorry she was. But the Queen was not amused.

"Someone take this guard to the tower," she ordered, clicking her fingers.

"Why am I being sent to the tower?"

"Because you're annoying."

"Is it a crime to be annoying?" the guard asked carefully, hoping the answer would be no.

"No."

Phew.

"But it is a crime to ask if it's a crime to be annoying," the Queen said. "I just made that up. Rather good, isn't it?" She clicked her fingers again and the guard was gone, taken to the tower to await her fate.

The Queen cast an eye over the crowd gathered in the square to see if there were any whispers of *give her a break*, *bad show* and *that's not very fair*. But the crowd wanted to LIVE, so not one of them said or did anything.

The Queen, satisfied, turned back to the whimpering boy.

"Explain yourself," she said, stretching out her leg and kicking him on the nose. "Why did you trap one of Brutalia's Royal Ravens?"

Let's get one thing clear: before this point they were simply **ravens**. Had they been **Royal Ravens**, the Queen might have fed them or popped little crowns on their heads. But they were scruffy and no one cared for them at all, which is why they had become so hungry they'd attacked Weed's fruit garden. One of the ravens (the one who fancied the nutty thalamus) had got tangled in the bird-proof netting. The flurry and panic that followed had alerted a guard, who had then alerted the Queen, who had decided there and then that the ravens were royal property and that the boy was in deep, deep trouble. Weed just hoped the Queen didn't punish him for growing his own fruit, which was also a crime.

"You've been growing your own fruit!" she squealed.

"We're so hungry," the boy said. "Do you know what it's like to have a hunger that gnaws at your insides? Do you know what it's like to hear your little sister crying herself to sleep at night?"

"No." (Everyone knew the Queen didn't have a soft side, but anything was worth a shot.) "So you were growing fruit, hoping to lure my Royal Ravens so that you could make raven pie?"

"I just wanted the fruit actually," Weed said. "I never meant to catch a raven."

The Queen threw her head back and gave a strange fake laugh, making her shoulders jig up and down to show that, finally, she was amused.

"*Why wouldn't* you want a raven for a pie? Don't you like pie?"

(The way she said **pie** – drawn out and tempting, like a sigh: *piiiiiigh* – made the hungry boy's mouth water.)

"A raven in a **pie**. A raven ***pie***. Are you telling me you wouldn't want **pie**...?"

"Well—"

"**Pie**," she said again for no reason.

"I would, but—"

"**Pie**."

"Yes, but—"

"*Pie*."

He could take it no more. "Of course I'd love raven pie!"

And the Queen shouted: **"PUNISHABLE BY DEATH!"**

The crowd wanted to gasp but couldn't, for obvious reasons. And the King, who had said nothing because he never did, belched as he changed position in his chair. For any ordinary citizen of Brutalia, belching in public could get you killed.

Brutalia is not a fair place.

That was the sad thought of a boy called Mort as he left the square that afternoon. All night he tossed and turned, haunted by the cruelty of the fate of his friend, Weed Millet. Nightmares washed over him in giant waves and he hardly slept a wink.

But at least you finally got to meet the main character.

CHAPTER THREE
THE EXECUTION

"That boy's got brains."

*"He got caught. Clever people
don't get caught, do they?"*

*"To eat, you FOOL. Brains to eat.
I wasn't going to drag him along
to our next quiz night."*

The following day, Mort walked miserably to the square and stood alongside his one-armed mother in the front row of the viewing area. He hated violence – hated it with his very soul – but Weed wanted him there as a friendly face to gaze at as he met his fate. Mort forced back the tears as his best friend was pulled on to the platform in front of him and gasped.

Weed's face was dark and slimy from sleeping on the mouldy prison floor, and there were cockroaches in his hair. He would have looked a hundred per cent swamp monster if it wasn't for his big chocolatey eyes, which he locked with Mort's average-sized green ones. Lumps formed in both their throats. Neither of them was certain how much longer Weed's throat would be in one piece.

The method of execution was decided by the Royal Executioner who, after the Queen and King, was the next most important person in Brutalia. He was not only chief murderer but also the Champion of Brutalia. It was his duty to make sure Brutalia didn't turn soft like the rest of the Salty Sea Islands, where people were happy, did yoga and didn't get their heads chopped off.

The current Royal Executioner was known as the

Brute. (Although all the executioners were given the same title, so he wasn't that special.) The Brute usually waited until everyone else was seated and the square was tense with anticipation before making an appearance. It was an attention-seeking thing.

Mort rolled his eyes – not because he wanted the Brute to hurry up and kill his friend. He was just bored with the Brute's **BIG DRAMATIC ENTRANCE**. He did it *all* the time, even at family dinners. The Brute, whose real name was Bob, was Mort's uncle. And Mort thought he was a bit of a twit.

Mort's eye-roll was interrupted by the sudden and undignified parp of one hundred horns. The Queen and King were brought in on sofas mounted on poles, carried by women and children whose knees buckled under the weight, although not one of them dared to complain...

Mort should have been watching the royal arrival, as every obedient citizen must, but he couldn't tear himself from Weed's eyes. They were pleading for help, but help wasn't something Mort was in a position to offer. What could he do?

BANG! BANG! BANG!

The crowd hushed at the familiar noise of the Royal Executioner's knuckle stick pounding the stage.

The knuckle stick was a knobbly cane, riddled with bumps that looked like knuckles. Mort gulped. Surely the Brute wasn't going to knuckle his best friend to death? That would be **so barbaric**, **so evil**, **so brutal**. So yeah, he probably was.

The Brute stood in the centre of the stage and held out his arms for adoring applause. The crowd reluctantly cheered as the guards held up *CLAP NOW* signs. Long after the noise had died down, the Brute remained still, eyes closed, arms wide open, soaking up (what he believed to be) the love of the people.

"Get on with it!" shouted the Queen.

The Brute bowed in her direction. "Your Royal Highnesses," he said, "today we are gathered to witness the punishment by death handed down to Weed Millet, the baker's boy, for his heinous crime –" (the guards held up *BOO NOW* signs) – "of ensnaring a Royal Raven –" (BOO NOW) – "for the purpose of placing it in a pie!" *(BOO NOW,*

BOO NOW.) "And so, in considering a suitable death for this evil boy—"

"Adult," the Queen corrected quickly. "He's thirteen and a half."

"—a suitable death for this adult, most certainly aged thirteen and a half, I pondered long and hard. With both the criminal and the crime in mind, I searched my encyclopaedia of executions to find the perfect form of—"

"Get on with it or I'll send you to the tower!"

The Brute looked at the Queen and saw from the expression on her face that she meant it, so he coughed loudly and prepared to deliver his decision.

"I declare that you, Weed Millet, shall be put to death by..."

ARGGGHHHHH

(???)

ARGGGHHHHHH

(Was it a raven?)

ARGGGHHHHHHH

(Was it Weed whimpering in fear?)

ARGGGHHHHHHHH

(What was it?)

ARGGGHHHHHHHHH

(Seriously, what was it?)

Mort looked at Weed but Weed was still very much alive, so it wasn't a terrible gargling death rattle...

No, Mort realized. It was coming from the Brute!

ARGGGHHHHHHHHHHH

(Actually it was getting a bit boring now.)

The Brute stumbled forward. The knuckle stick fell from his hands and the monstrous man clutched at his chest as he repeated the awful sound over and over, eyes boggling like ping-pong balls in a bathtub, which the ravens appreciated.

ARGGGHHHHHHHHHHHH...
BONK.

The Royal Executioner lay flat on his face on the stage and the crowd cheered, finally giving him the adoring chant he'd always longed for. The official Body Carrier, who had been waiting in the wings to dispose of Weed, dragged the Royal Executioner off the stage.

"Oh, for Brutalia's sake," the Queen said, rising from her sofa and standing on the heads of two small children. "Who's next in line for Royal Executioner? Does the Brute have a child?"

There was no answer. As far as anyone knew, the Brute lived alone with a cat called Flossy, but cats don't have thumbs, and can't hold knuckle sticks, and therefore make pathetic executioners.

"A sibling then?" the Queen snapped, exasperated. "Does he have a brother or a sister?"

Mort looked up at his mum.

"I'm the sister of Bob the Brute," she said.

"OK, OK, so I hereby declare you – what's your name?"

"Avon Canal. Me and my husband, Kennet, are the town plumbers, Your Majesty."

"Not any more. Avon Canal, you are now Royal Executioner and you shall henceforth be known as the Brute. Excellent. Now get on with it."

The Queen sat down, some horns parped and the crowd cheered, because they knew they probably should.

"One small problem," Mort's mum said. "I've only got one arm."

The Queen was off her sofa again and back on to the heads of the struggling children.

"One arm? Why?"

"I lost it jousting."

"Jousting is a crime!" the Queen screamed.

"I was jousting for the royal team under your command," Mort's mum said very carefully. "We won, if you remember... You gave me a very fine medal."

A woman with one arm didn't have much more axe-wielding power than a cat called Flossy. For a moment it looked as if the Queen might sentence her to death, despite her jousting victory, just for the inconvenience Mrs Canal had caused her ... but she was getting fed up.

"Anyone else then? Do YOU have a child?"

Mort's mum gave Mort a push. "Yes, I have a son. He's here. His name is Mort."

"Is he complete? No missing bits and pieces?"

"He is complete," Avon said, nudging Mort towards the platform.

"Well, thank the gallows for that!" The Queen sighed. The crowd cheered. The Queen told them to shut up.

"Behold the new Royal Executioner – Mort the Brute!"

Mort – the hot, sad lump in his throat now turned to ice – climbed on to the stage in front of the crowd.

The Queen clapped her hands. "Now kill this boy and let's be done with it."

CHAPTER FOUR
MORT
THE BRUTE

"You know the saying – you are what you eat?"

"Yeah, I've heard that."

*"If our favourite food is eyeballs, would
that make us ... feathery flying eyeballs?"*

"Stop it. You're freaking me out."

One minute he was about to see his best friend executed, and the next ... he was **THE EXECUTIONER**.

Mort sat with his head in his hands. He couldn't believe what he'd just done.

What **HAD** he just done? **WHAT** had he just done? What had he just **DONE?** (It sounded bad, whichever way you looked at it.)

You think he killed his friend? What kind of a sick person are you?

No. **This** is what he did:

With a yell that sounded like the shriek of some inner demon, Mort had picked up the fallen knuckle stick and raised it in the air above Weed's head. Weed had begged and pleaded but Mort had ignored his friend's big, watery, chocolatey, innocent, frightened eyes... Instead he had turned to the crowd and said, "To mark my first act as Royal Executioner, I want to do something really nasty." (Up went the *CHEER NOW* signs.) "I will execute Weed Millet –" *(CHEER NOW)* – "but I need time to think of something despicable. Give me one week and I will give you a dazzling display, a bogglingly brutal bashing, demonstrating that I am Mort the Most Brutal Brute of Brutalia!"

"Finally a Brute with some imagination! I love it!" the Queen had yelled. "See you in a week, and it had better be good or we'll be appointing a new Royal Executioner to chop off *your* head!"

So **that's** what he'd gone and done.

On the one hand it was good news because Weed would live another week. On the other it was bad news, as Mort would have to kill his best friend in seven days' time. And pretty horribly too.

Mort was obviously joking about being the Most Brutal Brute of Brutalia, but he had to walk the walk now that he'd talked the talk. And, when he'd talked the talk, he'd sounded like a fully signed-up member of the Brutal Brigade.

The trouble was, Mort could never be a fully signed-up member of the Brutal Brigade because he was a fully signed-up member of the Pacifist Society of Brutalia (members: one). Being a pacifist meant he didn't believe in violence. Na-uh, no way, not even a quick punch or a finger-crunch. And murder was definitely out.

Mort was such a devoted pacifist that every day he recited a Pacifist Promise. It went as follows:

I, a member of the Pacifist Society of Brutalia, promise not to hurt anything.
(It wasn't very imaginative but keeping it simple made it easier to remember.)

And it wasn't just people he hated hurting. Mort was such a pacifist he struggled to shoo away the fruit flies from his daily ration of rotten potatoes in case he damaged one of their wings. And the only reason he ate rotten potatoes covered with fruit flies at all was because he refused to eat meat. It made home life hard because the rest of his family were definitely not pacifists. They ate whatever they could get their hands on – worms, spiders, rats – and were all pretty violent, as was normal.

Fighting was a Brutalia hobby – the only hobby that wouldn't get you thrown in prison. Mort's younger twin siblings, Gosh and Gee, regularly ambushed each other with punches to the gut. They tried to make it look like fun, but Mort always refused to play.

That's why his nickname was **Mort the Meek**.

Mort sat with his head in his hands for hours. So many hours, it was the next day. And he was still sitting with his head in his hands when Gosh and Gee entered the room, tangled together in a ball, fists flying.

"Join in!" said Gee, with an **OOF!** as Gosh hit him.

"Yeah! **OW!**" said Gosh. "Come on, it's fun. I've already lost two teeth. Brilliant!"

The sibling fight-ball rolled right into the dinner gong and their four fists flew out, banging it every couple of seconds. **BONG! BONG! BONG!** (It also happened to be a rather good sound for impending doom.)

How was he supposed to think about executing his best friend with this kind of racket going on?

"Stop it at once," Mort said.

Gosh and Gee knew Mort was more likely to send them to bed with a lavender-scented hot-water bottle than execute them. Nevertheless, they unwound and stood at Mort's feet like two dirty-faced eight-year-old ratbags, which is what they were.

"Do you want to join in, Mort?" they asked in unison.

"Absolutely not," he replied.

"Why won't you fight?" Gosh asked. "You're *the Brute* now!"

"People will think it's *strange* if you don't fight," Gee added.

"Uncle Bob used to walk about the square at night, thumping innocent people, to show he was a brutalist."

"If you don't do regular thumping, people might start asking questions."

"Questions like, 'Is he a big softy?' and, 'Is he up to the job?'"

"And what if they find out his nickname is Mort the Meek?"

(The twins were talking to each other now as if Mort wasn't there.)

"Mort the Meek is a bit of a dangerous nickname to have if you're the Royal Executioner."

"What if we say it's a joke nickname? Like:

Mort the Meek? *I don't think so!*

Mort the Meek? *Hardly!*

Mort the Meek? *Say that and he'll knock your block off!*

Mort the Meek? *Yeah, he's SO timid!*"

"I love sarcasm – it lets you get away with anything."

The twins laughed and then punched each other in the face. Mort sighed, collected their fallen teeth and left them to it.

He couldn't be gone long because, unless his kid brother and sister wanted to eat soup for the rest of their lives, he had to get their teeth back in position. A knocked-out tooth could be saved if you put it back in the hole within an hour. And a mouthwash made with marigold flowers helped with the healing process.

But to collect the flowers Mort the Meek would have to break some rules. Picking flowers was illegal – banned, of course, by the Queen, who was determined to be the most beautiful thing in Brutalia and saw flowers as hot competition. Nevertheless, Mort cultivated them in secret on the south side of the island where it was forbidden to go, because it's where the royal farmers grew crops for the palace. It was also where the sun shone – and sunbathing, even for a second, even by accident, was punishable by death.

Mort, careful not to be seen, made his way through the grimy backstreets and soggy side streets of Brutalia to the south side of the island, to where his marigolds grew near the edge of a rocky cliff. He picked them gently and, while he was picking them, he panicked because what Gosh and Gee had said was true – sooner or later he was going to have to get brutal.

The sun beat down.

"Even the sun can beat," Mort said glumly.

He sat among the beautiful flowers, trying to talk the caterpillars and snails into getting off the petals, and eventually flicking them, which wasn't like him. But he was feeling stressed. Not about his siblings' teeth or thumping random people. He was feeling stressed about Weed.

I'm going to be a Weed killer, which is kind of funny, Mort thought sadly, although it wasn't funny and he knew it.

He also knew that right at that moment Weed was sitting in slime, probably being tortured with some kind of irritating noise and being given a dinner of cockroach stew (a bucket of cockroaches thrown over the prisoner's head). Weed wouldn't be enjoying that at all, although he could eat the cockroaches if he managed to catch any, as he wasn't a vegetarian like Mort.

"What am I going to do?" Mort shouted down at the sea. "Tell me, what am I going to do?"

But the sea only had a saltwater solution, which is not the solution he was looking for. There was no inspiration to be found in its depths, no ideas bobbing on its choppy waves, no answers thrown up in the cutting spray. But the Salty Sea never had been a place of encouragement or hope; it was just a big grey burial ground.

All Brutalia's dead got tipped into the Salty Sea. And Weed would be next.

Sea Weed, that's quite funny, Mort thought miserably, before remembering, even more miserably, *and it's because of me that he's going to end up there.*

Tears blurred his vision, making funny shapes of the landscape behind him, and of the seascape ahead of him, and of the shorescape right below him. And, for a moment, he thought he saw someone down beneath the cliff on the rocky beach, where the sea hit the land in great big slaps. Surely nobody would be bonkers enough to go to Brutalia's edge? No one living, anyway. Mort wiped away his tears and stood up to get a better view.

He saw the violent swell of the steel-grey water whirlpooling in the bay and ... and ... and ... a boat. *A boat!* And a boy. *A boy!* And a body. *Yuk ... a body...*

How strange! All bodies were supposed to be tipped into the brine from the highest cliff on the north side of Brutalia, which plummeted directly into the water, not put on a boat.

If Mort had to practise being brutal, maybe dealing with a law-breaker was a good place to start. It was going to be hard but he'd reach deep down into his soul – because, if there was any darkness in him, it was bound to be lurking there. But how did you reach into your soul? How did you get to that place inside you where your demons lie? Probably not by standing among pretty marigold flowers.

Mort quickly popped his petals in a pouch and, avoiding the royal fields where farmers patrolled armed with spiky gardening equipment, he made his way down to the ugly rocky shore to get brutal.

CHAPTER FIVE
OH NO!

"I'm so hungry I could murder something!"

"Yeah, but we don't do murder. We're not birds of prey."

*"Well, maybe we **should** be birds of pray.*
Come on, put your wings together and say after me:
'Dear Food Gods, if you're listening, please bring
us some fresh eyeballs or a tasty spleen...'"

"Oh, Rav ... you've got your homophones*
mixed up again."

---

* Homophones are words that sound the same, like HARE and
HAIR. That's why spelling is important, which you'll know if
you've ever tried to wash your hare.

Getting brutal isn't that easy if you're a pacifist.

You've got to know how to fight for a start, and to do that you need to be able to make a decent fist. Mort didn't know how to do that, because there's no fist in pacifist. Hang on – paci-*fist*. OK, so there is, but let's move on.

Mort hid behind a rock to gather his thoughts and to work out how to fold his fingers into a bunch of knuckles (he didn't know where to put his thumbs). He couldn't do it. He couldn't do any of it because the Pacifist Promise was ringing in his ears.

I, a member of the Pacifist Society of Brutalia, promise not to hurt anything.

As it turned out, it was a good thing he stopped to think rather than running right into a fight, and not just because his thumbs were in the wrong place. The little figure on the shore wasn't alone. Another person, who had probably just nipped into a sea cave to have a quick wee, suddenly appeared alongside the boy. It was a man, as thin as a stick but taller than anyone else in

Brutalia. It was the Body Lugger!

Mort scurried to a rock closer to the sea and watched the man and boy try to steady the tiny boat as it rolled and bucked on the angry wash.

Mort crept over to an even closer rock and gasped. The body was none other than his uncle, Bob! Uncle Bob's lifeless limbs kept flinging themselves out of the boat every time it was nudged by the uneasy sea. It looked as if he was throwing punches, which he would have been pleased about.

Mort crept closer. And closer. Until he'd run out of closer and was right there, standing on the rocky edge of Brutalia, watching the boat sail away with Uncle Bob and the law-breaking Body Luggers. Why hadn't they thrown Bob into the Salty Sea from the Great North Rock like they were supposed to? What were they up to?

In case you hadn't worked it out, Body Luggers hurled the dead into the sea. That was their job. They were at the very bottom of Brutalia's horrible chain of death, which went like this:

The Queen and King told someone they were going

to die, **then**

the Royal Executioner killed them, **then**

the Body Carrier carried them away, **then**

the Body Lugger lugged them to the edge of cliff and hurled 'em off, **then...**

There were no more **thens**, unless you were a raven.

If you were a raven, you'd say then great – that's dinner sorted!

Lugging was the least glorious of all the jobs. There was no audience, no parping of horns and no cheering. In fact, lugging was a rotten-stinking job to have.

It was nobody's fault that bodies got rotten and stinky after a while, but everyone avoided the Body Lugger and his family like the plague. They rarely came into the town but, when they did, people scattered like cockroaches. The rumour was that Body Luggers never spoke because their tongues had frozen from the horror of their task. And, if you touched a Body Lugger, your arm would fall off.

Mort's mum once joked that she hadn't lost her arm in a joust at all but because she'd bumped into Plop Assunder, the needle-thin Body Lugger, in the marketplace. Mort, just like his parents and his siblings, had laughed and laughed at the time. But he wasn't laughing now.

Why?

Because some *weird stuff* was going on.

And then some *wind stuff* was going on.

A sudden brisk breeze snatched the pouch of marigold petals from Mort's hand and tossed it on to the gravelly beach. It was an annoying turn of events but led nicely to the bit that's about to happen, and you wouldn't want to miss that. *(Thank you, wind.)*

Mort left his clifftop spot and scrambled down the steep escarpment on to the shore. He found his marigold pouch wedged between two stones. But they weren't stones... They were the feet of the Body Lugger's boy, who had been well camouflaged in his slate-grey rags. As Mort reached for his pouch, the kid stood on his knuckles.

"Ow!"

"Sorry, I didn't see you there."

"I was right in front of you!"

"And I was looking up at those ravens so, like I said,

I didn't see you."

Mort glanced up. There were indeed ravens. They had descended, hoping to pounce on a bit of Uncle Bob before he got shipped away. Now they were circling in disappointment just above their heads, looking for nits.

"Hang on a minute," Mort said. "You spoke! I thought you were mute, your tongue frozen from the horror of your task."

"That's just a rumour. It's true that Dad doesn't talk much, but only because he never has anything interesting to say. I'm Ono, by the way. Ono Assunder."

The boy held out a hand and Mort shook it.

"I'm Mort. Ono's a funny name."

"My dad was hoping for a boy. When I came out, he said, '*Oh no.*' It kind of stuck."

"So you're a girl then?" Mort said.

"Might be."

"You're not dressed like a girl."

"That's a stupid thing to say. I can dress how I want. I'm one of a kind."

Mort looked at the boy who might be a girl. She was a bit scrawny and had hair that was short and so matted with salt it was grey. She also had a little nose, thin lips and cloud-grey eyes.

"Ono comes from the Greek for 'name', which is handy," Ono said, breaking the silence.

"What does Mort mean?"

"Probably comes from the Latin word for death."

"Oh no..."

"Yes?"

"No, Ono – I meant **oh no!** I hate death. I don't want to have anything to do with death. Although it looks like I have no choice..."

Ono yawned and Mort wondered if it was too soon to be talking about deep and meaningful stuff with someone he'd only just met. Although there was one question he needed to ask.

"Ono, where are you taking Bob?"

"I can't tell you that, we've only just met!"

Mort nodded. It was a fair point.

"Just give it another minute," Ono said.

For another whole minute they didn't speak and moved only to fend off ravens who thought they might offer up some eyeballs.

"It's probably been a minute now," said Mort, who had been counting to sixty in his head.

"Yeah. OK, so I'll tell you, but only because I've known you for some time," Ono said, placing a trusting hand on Mort's shoulder. "The truth is, we haven't lugged anyone off a cliff for ages. We've been taking them to our island and giving them a proper burial."

"That's against the law!" Mort gasped.

"No one ever talks to us," Ono said, "so no one will ever know."

"But *I* just talked to you."

"Yeah, but you won't say anything. It's not like what happens to the old executioner is any business of yours."

No business of yours? Hang on a minute!

Mort felt suddenly and surprisingly loyal to Uncle Bob. Or maybe he felt that Ono was getting a bit too big for her raggedy boots. Mort puffed up his chest.

"It *is* my business actually. He's my uncle. And I'm the new Royal Executioner. I should probably get a bit brutal with you to teach you a lesson."

Ono shrank back.

"That's right." Mort gulped and tried to sound mean. "You should be scared."

"You don't look scary," Ono said, stepping forward again, head to one side like a curious chicken.

"I'm just making you think I'm not scary so that it's easier to scare you. Aha!"

"So you absolutely promise me you're horrible then, even if you look like a bit of a wimp?"

"My heart is black with the breath of demons."

(Mort thought he was doing quite well.)

Ono's nose wrinkled in disbelief. "Why were you picking flowers then?"

Her mouth twitched. So did Mort's. Before they knew it they were laughing and laughing and laughing. And Mort had to admit that his heart wasn't black with the breath of demons and he did like flowers a lot. Uncle Bob would not have been proud.

"If you like flowers, you should come to my place," Ono said. "We grow marigolds twice the size of those, and herbs and exotic plants."

"Where do you live?" Mort said.

"Just the other side of the horizon, on Dead Man's Island."

They looked over at the horizon. On it bobbed Plop

Assunder's boat, returning to collect his one-of-a-kind kid.

"I'd better go," Ono said, grabbing hold of Mort's arm. "When they need us to lug, they send a pigeon. If you ever want to get hold of me, just look for the pigeon with the red tag on its leg. Call it with three short whistles, and send it off again with three more."

Without another word, Ono scurried along the shore and waded into the stinging sea, ready to jump aboard the little boat. Mort wanted to jump in too. He wanted to see a place called Dead Man's Island where marigolds grew as big as your head. He wanted to spend more time with the curious Ono. But, if he dallied any longer, Gosh and Gee's teeth wouldn't set properly.

He hurried home, up over the slippery rocks, past the royal crops and into the greasy backstreets and slimy side streets of Brutalia, where he was immediately hit in the ears by the familiar sound of people beating each other up.

Fists went **OOOF!**

Kicks went **CRACK!**

And something went **SPLAT!**
(Probably best not to ask.)

Mort dodged the skirmishes and scurried through the dark lanes, dreaming of a sea breeze, a field of flowers and a strange girl called Ono, whom he hadn't been able to punch.

CHAPTER SIX
THE MILLETS

"We could always attack the humans."

"No way! They'd give us a knuckle sandwich."

"Yum ... knuckle sandwich..."

It was hard getting Gosh and Gee to sit still. They were wrigglers. Even in their sleep they punched at the ceiling and scrabbled around in the bedsheets, their dreams full of fights and good ways to lose teeth.

As Mort was trying to get Gee's tooth back in the hole, Gosh swung her arm across Gee's throat.

"KAPOW!" she yelled, extremely proud of herself.

Gee then kicked Gosh in the kneecaps with a **CRUNCH**.

"This is ridiculous!" Mort yelled. "Stay still, both of you, or I'll…"

"What? Make me a daisy chain?" Gee laughed.

"Clean my room for me?" Gosh giggled.

"Or how about I put you before the Queen and King?" Mort snarled.

Gosh and Gee fell silent… Then they laughed their heads off and started chanting, "Mort the Meek, Mort the Meek, Mort the Meek," over and over, and very LOUDLY, which meant anyone who might be passing in the street below would hear.

As it happens, an unpleasant man called Snit

Parlot was passing in the street below and *did* hear. Unfortunately Snit was a dealer in secrets for the Queen: his job was to listen into private conversations and pass on the juicy details.

And so the plot thickens.

"You're right, I'd never put you before the Queen and King," Mort sighed. "But please don't shout Mort the Meek like that. Someone might hear."

OOPS!

"And, if someone did, I'd probably be challenged."

YEP!

"And if I was challenged I'd have to do something really brutal to prove that I can be Royal Executioner."

HE'S GOT THE HANG OF IT!

"And I'm just not a brutal person."

YOU'RE NOT KIDDING!

"And the Queen will kill me."

OH DEAR...

Gosh and Gee felt so bad for putting Mort in danger that they shut up while their teeth were being reaffixed and gargled their marigold mouthwash without a fuss. It was almost as if they weren't scrap-happy ratbags at all. But they totally were so, as soon as Mort left the room, Gee knocked Gosh's tooth out and they laughed themselves sick.

It was the next day, just five periods of twenty-four hours before Weed's execution. The ravens rumbled above and the sun probably shone on the other side of the island, but the streets that wormed between Brutalia's leaning buildings were shady and grim. It could well have been night-time, and Mort, exhausted from the emotions of the day before, would have slept in until noon had it not been for some jarring noises.

Mort knew what those sounds were: they were jars smashing against the other side of the kitchen wall.

His mother and father were having a row with the next-door neighbours again, although luckily it was at their place this time. From the clanging and thwanging, it sounded as if they were also throwing cutlery. It was his mother's weapon of choice. She started screaming obscenities about forks, which meant things were hotting up. Mort had to get out of there before she called for family reinforcement.

"Mort! Mort! Bring the spare spoons – they're in the box on top of the cupboard— **OOF!**"

Mort, pretending he hadn't heard, grabbed his coat and slipped out of the back door.

He was going to see Weed. He had dreamed of him, lonely and slimy and awaiting his fate. The slime and fate things were pretty unfixable but Mort thought he might be able to relieve the loneliness bit, because as Royal Executioner he was the only one with permission to visit. He decided to stop by Weed's house on the way to see how his family was bearing up.

Before he even reached the Millets' front door, Mort was met by a waft of the wonderful smell of warm dough.

It was always woven into Weed's clothes and hair – the smell, not the dough. Of course, Weed didn't smell of it now because he was in a dungeon and smelling of rat wee. But in the good old days, before ravens got caught in fruit nets, Weed was Mort's most delicious-smelling friend, and Weed always brought him offcuts from the bakery – bits of doughnuts or bagels or croissants that his parents made for the palace.

With a tear in his eye, Mort knocked on the Millets' door, not knowing how he'd be received. In less than a week he would be disposing of their child and most parents don't take kindly to that sort of thing. Mr Millet was a big man and once upon a time he might have given Mort a right good thump. Not now, though. He'd be sentenced to death for hurting the Royal Executioner. Mr Millet had also gone weak with grief and couldn't throw pastry, never mind a punch.

"Mort."

Weed's father filled the doorway with his bulky frame – tears in his eyes and flour on his face. His fingers were webbed with raw dough.

"Hi, Mr Millet," Mort said, with a gulp. "I just came to see how you were bearing up."

"Did you hear that?" Mr Millet shouted behind him at Mrs Millet. "The Royal Executioner called me a bear! As if murdering our son isn't enough, he's insulting me too!"

There was silence. Mrs Millet wasn't in a position to speak because she was face down in a mound of dough, and had been all morning. She was so full of rage she had shaken herself quite mad. She was a boiling, shuddery lump of fury. Beneath the dough, she was like a volcano about to blow.

"I just meant I wanted to see how you were coping."

Mr Millet's face softened. "Oh right. Well, thanks for asking. We're fine..." His shoulders started shaking and he began to sob quietly. His salty tears mixed with the flour on his cheeks, creating a salty, doughy face-pack. He clearly wasn't fine.

"Come in," he blubbed.

Mort entered the house. Weed's little sister, Semolina, was in the corner, making figures out of dough. Mort tried to ignore the strange image of Mrs Millet bent over a table with her head in some raw bread.

"I'm on my way to see Weed," he said. "Do you want me to pass on a message?"

"Yeah. You tell him that we love him," Mr Millet sobbed, "and he's our special boy –" (more tears) – "and we can't imagine going on without him..." (*drip, drip, drip*) "and we just don't know what to do –" (where were those tears coming from?) – "and I'll never run out of tears for him –" (looked like he was telling the truth) – "and— *HOOOOOWL!*"

After his cry of anguish, Mr Millet fell forward and face-planted in a pile of dough next to his wife. It seemed to be what they did.

Suddenly the living-room door behind them gave a sharp **CRACK!**

The door was splitting! Pushed from the other side by a great force.

"What's happening?" Mort cried.

"*Frrr-nnn-mmmmmrrr-f,*" said Mr Millet from inside the dough.

"What?"

"*Frrr-ffurff-irff!*"

What a ridiculous thing to say, Mort thought, and he opened the door to see for himself.

KABLOOOF!

He was hit in the face, neck, chest, thighs and feet by a giant ball of bulging dough. It had filled the whole of the living room and was quickly expanding into the kitchen.

Mr Millet, who had dragged his face off the table,

said flatly: "Dough's risen, darling."

Mrs Millet said nothing.

In their anguish, the Millets hadn't been fighting (which was the norm). They'd been baking. They'd been baking a lot. Mort thought they'd gone quite mad with grief and left, snatching a small bag of doughnuts from the worktop as he went.

You never knew when you might need a little sweetener.

CHAPTER SEVEN
THE CELL
OF DOOM

*"I don't know what prisoners complain
about - there's plenty to eat in the dungeons."*

"There's nothing down there but rats and fleas."

*"If you use a little imagination, you've got
yourself rat-atouille and fleas-burgers."*

Moans and groans drifted through the gloomy corridors as people cried out in mild discomfort. Numb bum from sitting on the cold stone floors was a common complaint. Also trapping your fingers in the bars – they were actually a lot closer together than they looked. Prisoners weren't usually tortured in Brutalia's prison in case they got used to it, which would make public floggings a bit boring.

The Queen liked her floggings to go:

WHIP!

OW!

Not:

WHIP!

Yawn, are we doing this fifty lashes thing or not?

WHIP!

Was there a mosquito on me?

WHIP!

Is that all you've got?

But the Cell of Doom was different. It's where those due to be executed were held. As if their fate wasn't depressing enough, the Queen liked them to be especially miserable in the lead-up to the Big Chop. The room was pitch-black and the doomed prisoner's feet were chained to the floor, so that the rats could sharpen their teeth on their toes while they slept. But they never slept because a horn blower parped every ten minutes to make sure they didn't.

The Cell of Doom was heavily guarded by a man called Brutus, who was as tall as a door and as wide as a wall.

"Who goes there?" Brutus roared as Mort approached.

"It's Mort the Brute," Mort said boldly. "The Royal Executioner. Stand aside so I may view the vile prisoner."

"On what business?" Brutus snarled.

"On no business of yours!" Mort retorted.

There was an awkward silence.

"It's about now that people pay me off with something like a bag of doughnuts," Brutus whispered.

"Oh right! How about I pay you off with some doughnuts then?" Mort said, plucking one out and waving the rest of the sugary delights before his face.

"That's more like it," Brutus said, snatching the bag and shuffling off into the gloom.

"Well played," said a weak voice in the darkness.

"Weed?"

Mort struck a match and held it up to the close-together bars. It was pitch-black and he couldn't see his friend in the stinking cell behind them. Weed's face popped up from nowhere and pressed against the bars.

"Oh, what have they done to you?" Mort cried.
"Have they grilled you?"

"No."

"Then you have a horrible disease, Weed. Your face
– it's covered with black stripes!"

"Could it be the shadows of the bars on my face,
from the candlelight, Mort?" Weed asked.

Indeed it was, and how they laughed – HA HA!

It was a sound the prison wasn't accustomed to.
The walls threw it round and round like a hot potato,
and the laugh lasted much longer than its original
HA HA! The boys grinned at each other and tears
glistened in their eyes.

"I needed that laugh," Weed said, poking his fingers
carefully through the bars so as not to get them stuck.
Mort touched them with his own fingertips, before
slipping Weed the doughnut.

"I bring this, and love from your parents."

"How are they bearing up?"

"Not good."

"Go on, tell me," Weed said.

"Baking mad," Mort said sadly.

"Oh no..."

"Speaking of which, I met someone called Ono," Mort said brightly, trying to steer the subject away from the Millets. He didn't want to have to tell Weed about their strange, doughy face-dunking. "Ono Assunder, the Body Lugger's child."

"But the luggers don't speak."

"Yes, they do."

"Did your arm fall off?"

"No, that's just a rumour. And there's some good news about you dying—"

Short, blunt footsteps rang on the stony floors. Someone was coming.

"Raven pie!" Mort yelled suddenly. **"I'll show you how to say sorry for raven pie, you snivelling little grot. I'm going to kill you in a really horrible way!"**

"I thought you said it was good news," Weed whispered, rather hurt.

"Shh," Mort hushed. **"And, by the time I've finished with you, you're going**

to wish you were dead!"

A man arrived, raised a horn and:

PARP!

He then lowered the instrument, nodded at them both and disappeared back up the tunnel.

"That was close," Mort said. "Who was that guy?"

"The Every-ten-minute Horn Blower. So what's the good news about me dying?" Weed's pleading eyes looked like pools of dark chocolate in the dim light.

"Ono told me they haven't pushed anyone off a cliff into the sea for ages. They're going to give you a proper burial, in the ground, on an island."

"That's *good* news?"

"It means you won't be raven food or end up at the bottom of the Salty Sea with an octopus living in your skull."

"I was kind of hoping you were going to say that I wasn't going to die at all."

"Ah. Yeah. I see how you might have thought that..."

Weed pulled his fingertips back through the bars and slid his whole body into the darkness of his cell like a snail until Mort could no longer see him. He could only hear the clank of the ankle chains scraping the stone floor, binding Weed to his rotten cell and to his fate.

Bind Weed, that's kind of funny, Mort said, realizing right away that it wasn't. Especially not to anyone who doesn't know that bindweed is a kind of plant. (Thank goodness you do.)

"But what choice is there?" Mort said despairingly.

"You could try not killing me." Weed's voice definitely had some grumpiness in it. It looked like prison hadn't quite broken his spirit.

"Bye, Weed. I'll try to visit you again."

"If you want." Weed sighed, and it suddenly seemed a long time ago that the laughter of two best friends had ricocheted round the cell. "Wait!"

Mort stopped and Weed came up close again.

"Do me a favour. Tell my parents to stop baking. If the Queen and King find out they've baked more than their rationed amount, they'll end up in here with me."

"I will," Mort said, with a sense of purpose.

"And, if you want a sense of purpose," Weed added, "why don't you think about not *killing* me a bit more?"

Mort stepped out of Brutalia's prison and right into a brawl that had begun at the grocery stall. Fists and vegetables were flying. And vegetable-flavoured insults.

"You knobbly parsnip!"

"NO ONE calls me a parsnip!"

"You've got a beetroot-bum for a face!"

"NO ONE says I've got a beetroot-bum for a face!"

"You're a radish short of a picnic!"

"I don't even like radishes in my picnics. I don't like picnics!"

It wasn't clever. It wasn't funny. And it wasn't for any reason anyone could remember. Most fights in Brutalia were utterly pointless.

Mort stayed well out of it but didn't disappear altogether in case a fresh vegetable rolled his way across the cobbles. He could do with a change from rotten potatoes.

A rotten potato rolled his way across the cobbles.

Come on, that's just not fair, Mort thought. But he leaned down to pick it up. In Brutalia you couldn't ignore free food, no matter what state it was in.

Out of nowhere, a raven swooped down, speared the rotten potato with its beak and flew away. Mort growled before telling himself he'd just lost a potato he didn't have, so he couldn't complain. But something bugged him, and it wasn't the maggot crawling up his right foot.

Since when did ravens eat potatoes? It wasn't the first time he'd noticed the ravens acting **weird**.

They used to keep out of people's way, sitting high up on the tops of the towers, occasionally flapping out to sea like charred paper on the wind... Recently they'd begun circling lower, getting tangled in people's hair (not to mention fruit nets), and, whereas they used to be fairly quiet, there was now a lot of squawking and squabbling and scrapping. They reminded Mort a bit of Gosh and Gee fighting over the last roast rat leg at the dinner table.

No one had ever fought him for the last rotten potato. Until now. It was almost as if bodies weren't being dumped at sea any more and the ravens needed to look for food elsewhere... Mort remembered Ono's dead-body confession and scratched his chin. But his scratching was interrupted.

"Not joining in the fight, *Mort the Brute?*"

Mort turned to see Malc Clam, who was not only a man whose name was the same backwards, but also the Queen's personal bodyguard.

Malc was solid muscle. He could twitch every part of himself he was so muscly and making his earlobes dance was his favourite party trick.

"Join in? No, not me," Mort said, standing as tall as he could and gazing at the cluster of people before them, shouting rude vegetable names.

"Why not? I thought you were supposed to be a brutalist. Real brutalists can't resist a fight."

"But this is a fight about vegetables. Pathetic! If I get involved in a fight, I want it to be a proper one."

"Good," said Malc. "Because you've got one."

Mort held his nerve and tried not to sweat. "What do you mean?"

Malc Clam leaned down and put his face right up

to Mort's. (Urgh, the stories were true – his breath did smell of sun-dried seafood.)

"Thing is, we heard a rumour that your nickname is Mort the Meek. And you wouldn't get a nickname like Mort the Meek unless it was true."

"It might be a sarcastic nickname," Mort said quickly. "Like Mort the Meek – *oh yeah, he's SO meek right now.*"

"In that case, you won't mind a fight. Here, the day after tomorrow, midday. And, by the way, you'll be fighting the Queen's least favourite tiger."

"WHAT?"

This was terrible news. Mort couldn't kill the tiger, for two and a half reasons.

1.   In a **Man v. Tiger** fight the tiger usually wins.

2.   Mort was a pacifist, so obviously he didn't
     want to kill **anything**.

2 ½ . Mort felt sorry for the tiger being the Queen's
     least favourite tiger, which meant she didn't care
     if it was killed, which was, you know, sad.

The whole thing was so ludicrous, it was almost as if
someone had made it up.

CHAPTER EIGHT
SCAREDY CAT

"Hey, I'm on a seafood diet. I see food and I eat it!"

"But we haven't seen food for days."

"It's a joke."

"You're telling me...!"

It was four days until Weed met his fate. But, right now, Mort was more concerned with his own – the very next day he was probably going to suffer tiger bites. Which are worse than mosquito bites, if you were wondering...

Mort's only chance of survival was the book he held in his hands. A book that once belonged to the Witch.

She wasn't really a witch – she was just an old woman who liked making medicines with plants. But that didn't matter. The truth never mattered when the Queen decided she wanted a big show. And no show was bigger than a trial that could end in DEATH!

The evidence hadn't look good:

★ Her name was Mags, probably short for Maggots, which sounded **witchy**.

★ She made healthy drinks with plants, which stank of **witchery**.

★ She had long grey hair with green tips, which looked **witch-ish**.

★ She was in top-to-bottom good health, and no one in Brutalia was in good health, so clearly...

She was a witch!

In case you're interested this was the truth:

★ Mags was short for Maggie, not Maggots.

★ Those potions? Nothing but nutritious smoothies.

★ Mags was healthy because she knew how to get the best nutrition from the few plants that grew in Brutalia's decaying corners and she made sure she got the right amount of sleep and exercise every day.

★ She hated the idea of being a boring old lady so experimented with hair dye, hence the green tips.

The only reason Mags came to be standing in front of the Queen and King at all was because of that slimeball, Snit Parlot. He'd been standing by her window as she went about making her herbal concoctions one day.

"Camomile flower or forget-me-not flower, which am I going to use?"

It's a shame that she was in the habit of talking to herself because, if she'd just said all of that in her head, Snit wouldn't have crept away with half-heard words and completely the wrong end of the stick.

Mort remembered how Mags had stood there at the trial, more radiant than a ten-year-old despite being seventy-seven, thanks to her daily routine of green tea and push-ups.

"You said it with your very own witchy lips!" the Queen had shrieked. "**Witch am I**. It's a confession."

"*Which*, not *witch*. I never said I was a witch."

"You just said it again. **I was a witch!**"

"I'm just trying to spell it out for you."

"**SPELL it out**. Did you hear that?"

The crowd had booed because guards had held up their big *BOO NOW* signs.

"I guess that's me dead then," the old woman had said.

"You can predict the future! Because you're a **WITCH!** I hereby declare you guilty and—"

"**PUNISHABLE BY DEATH!**"

Mags had shouted.

Mort remembered how the Queen's mouth had suddenly sucked inwards as if she was trying to swallow her own face.

"Those are MY words!" she'd shrieked. "You stole them from me without even touching me. **YOU ARE A WITCH!"**

"I think we've established that, you daft bat," the old woman replied and the crowd had cheered at a point when they weren't supposed to, which meant no food rations for three days.

The Queen had been utterly furious that Mags hadn't quivered with fear. In fact, the old lady's eyes had sparkled as she was led away, and Mort had been saddened that someone with such a love for life wasn't going to live much longer. Uncle Bob had carried out the Queen's orders the following day.

Royal Executioners got to keep anything belonging to their unfortunate ... clients, and Uncle Bob had a giant chest in his house full of stuff. It was there that Mort found Mags's handwritten book entitled FORAGING FOR NATURE STUFF.

Inside, Mags had written descriptions of plants,

what they did and where they could be found. FORAGING FOR NATURE STUFF is where Mort developed his interest in flowers. And it's how he learned about the plants on the south of the island.

As he now stood, looking out over the fields where those very plants grew, crouching suddenly when the crop guards came near, he remembered Mags with affection. He was also looking for a flower called **Coleus canina**, otherwise known as 'Scaredy-cat'.

To human nose it does not smell
But animals sniff it very well.
Unmistakably the scent reminds
Of foulness that comes from doggy behinds.
Cats will run, run, run away
With one small squirt of smelly spray.
So if you want to scare off cats I'd recommend it.

(Admittedly this did sound a bit witchy. I mean, who talks like that!)

Mort remembered seeing flowers a bit like the ones Mags had drawn – long stalks with purple heads – further down the fields, closer to the rocky shore.

He ran as fast as he could, skipping on the loose stones as the land bowed towards the water. He stopped just shy of the cliff edge, where he paused for a moment to look out over the Salty Sea. Somewhere just beyond the horizon was a place called Dead Man's Island and an interesting new friend called Ono Assunder.

Ono had said he could make contact if he wanted to. And maybe he would. Or maybe he wouldn't – he might be tiger food just after noon the next day.

Mort found the **Coleus canina** flowers and picked them all. He was going to need a lot, and even a lot might not be enough. He also needed lemon balm and rosemary to mash with them. It really was quite lucky that these plants grew on the island, because if they didn't Mort would most certainly die, and we're only halfway through the story.

At noon the next day, Mort the Brute stood in a fighting ring as the midday bell rang out across Brutalia. It rang and rang and rang, because there was no one to stop it. No crowds, no *CHEER NOW* signs, not even a pigeon. This was between Mort, the Queen and Warren.

That's right, Warren the tiger.

Sitting on the back of a small child, the Queen made herself comfortable by wriggling around.

"Mort the Brute, we have yet to see you carry out an execution. And, if you are as brutal as you claim, I look forward to it greatly. However, it has come to my attention that you have been taunted with the word..." The Queen reached deep into her lungs so she could project the next utterance with the power and disgust it deserved. **"MEEK!"**

"It was sarcasm," Mort said boldly.

"You just made that up."

"Sure, I just made up sarcasm..." Mort said, rolling his eyes without thinking.

"So you DID make it up!" the Queen said, sucking her teeth.

"No, that was *sarcasm*."

"THAT'S ENOUGH!"

The Queen stood up and sat down again, the child-chair went *OOF!* and the Queen clicked her fingers at Malc Clam, who was standing in the shadows behind.

Malc led Warren, muzzled and mean, into the ring.

Mort stood in one corner of the ring and the now unmuzzled Warren prowled towards him. His great nose twitched and his eyes itched with the anticipation of attack (Warren's, not Mort's).

This was no time for fear or for running away, which is what he really wanted to do (Mort, not Warren). He just hoped that the floral mush he'd rubbed all over his body and sewn into the lining of his clothes would be enough to repel the creature.

Warren came one step closer and Mort, realizing that as a fearless Brute he should probably have made the first move, quickly moved forward two steps.

The tiger stopped and cocked his head to the side as if to say, *Ah, so that's your game!* and moved three steps forwards and one to the left.

Mort moved right and one step forwards, placing him directly in front of the beast (or thereabouts).

"Checkmate!" Mort declared, though his heart was pounding.

Warren snarled, revealing razor-sharp teeth, and released a breath that smelled of a thousand dead rats. Then, tired of playing chess, the tiger lunged. He sprang silently into the air.

Time seemed to stand still and, for a while, Warren was suspended in mid-leap. Inside, Mort was trembling. But on the outside he had to show he was strong and fearless. He roared and gnashed his teeth, which were impressive for a child his age, thanks to

Mags's healthy-teeth potion. It would show the Queen that he was brave and capable of crunching an unripe apple without dentistry. But would it be enough to save him?

Warren descended from his mid-air leap, claws outstretched and jaws wide. It looked as if Mort was done for. But then the big cat caught a whiff of Mort the Most Brutal Brute.

*What **WAS** that smell?* The tiger's eyes boggled with alarm and, the closer he got to Mort, the stronger the pong ... until – *URGH, it smells like dogs' bottoms!*

The tiger flipped sideways to get away from the stench and fell badly on to his side, skidding across the stage. He was frankly too disgusted to give killing Mort another shot and instead started to lick his sore paw.

Mort stood, eyes wide with relief and disbelief. It was over! He was alive, and without a cat scratch. What's more, he hadn't even had to hurt Warren, which would have been against the Pacifist Code. It couldn't have gone better!

"Well, you have shown you're brave, Mort the Brute—" the Queen began.

"Wait!" said Malc Clam (because you weren't really expecting it to be that easy, were you?). "That wasn't a display of brutalism, was it? He just stood there! Maybe he just got lucky. Warren might have had tummy ache. Maybe he was having an off day."

"Good point," the Queen said. "You didn't really *do* much, did you? *Soooo*, you will fight again tomorrow, at midday, against a Grot Bear. Goodbye."

The Queen tapped the child-chair, who crawled on hands and knees back to the palace.

Mort looked at Malc Clam, who was chuckling to himself.

"What have you got against me?" he asked.

"Nothing really. But every story needs a heartless meanie who holds grudges for no particular reason, and that's me. Bad luck."

Bad luck indeed.

A Grot Bear!

A GROT BEAR!

The Grot Bears (full name: Grotesque Bears) were creatures the Queen kept for fun. They were huge and beary, like monstrous teddies with tiny brains. But not all Grot Bears were the same. Some were lovers and others were fighters, and none of them had any self-control.

They lived in dark caves under the palace and the only time they saw the light was on Brutalia's Sports Day – a day when the whole island was forced to watch the Grot Bears compete against each other in games such as Fluffy Kitten Fight. Some Grots desperately wanted to stroke the fluffy kittens while others desperately wanted to eat them, so the strokers attacked the eaters and the eaters attacked the strokers.

It invariably ended in torn-off limbs.* It was always a horrible event. No one likes to see big grotesque bears or sweet cuddly kittens in pieces. Especially not a pacifist.

*No kittens were harmed in the making of this story.

CHAPTER NINE
DEAD MAN

"Remember that amazing meal we once had?"

"The feast of eyeballs?"

"No, the sailors' hands, remember?"

"Oh yeah. It was finger-licking good."

Life was over. Mort knew it and so did Malc Clam. Even the ravens must have known it, because one sat on Mort's head, tugging at his eyelashes, and there were more at his feet, tenderizing his toes with their beaks.

Mort began to think the writer of his story had it in for him because, after repelling a giant cat against the odds, he really deserved a break. But no, story writers are fiendish beasts, and this one gave him less than twenty-four hours off before making him face one of the most fearsome creatures on Brutalia. What chance did he have against a vicious Grot Bear or one that might crush him to death with love? There was nothing about that in FORAGING FOR NATURE STUFF. And he couldn't fight. He *couldn't*.

If right now you're shouting *FIGHT! FIGHT! FIGHT!* like a bloodthirsty ratbag, then stop and remember this: Mort was a *fully signed-up member of the Pacifist Society of Brutalia* and fighting went against everything he believed in. For a pacifist, hurting anything was off limits and violence was never the answer.

How could he draw blood from a creature that liked tearing off limbs because it knew no other way? He couldn't.

He was a pacifist through and through.

OR... OR... OR... (*every tale needs a crisis of identity*) **was he pretending to be a pacifist because, deep down, he was just PLAIN SCARED?**

Oooo-OOO-ooooo!

Mort thought about his nickname: **Mort the Meek**.

It sounded small. But that was minor and insignificant – absolutely tiny – compared to the full list of thesaurus results.

Another word for Meek was...

Timid.

Another word for Timid was...

Fearful.

Another word for Fearful was...

Cowardly.

Another word for Cowardly was...

Gutless.

Another word for Gutless was...

Let's just leave it there:

GUTLESS.

All this time Mort had thought he was just a really nice lad. Perhaps he was, in fact, gutless and everyone but him could see it. The more he thought about it, the more it sounded right: *Mort the Gutless*.

Yes. He admitted it: he was scared. Violence was wrong, but it also hurt.

"I am gutless!" he yelled at no one.

But yelling it at no one didn't change the fact that a Grot Bear would be waiting for him the following day. What was he going to do?

As if this story was written with saving Mort in mind, another bird appeared among the black ones now queuing to peck at his toes. It was small and grey, with a head that bobbed like a dad at a disco.

And importantly, there was a red tag on its leg... This was a sign. This was a **pigeon!**

By the time Mort realized it was a sign and a pigeon, it had moved away. But that's OK, because all he had to do was whistle three short whistles. Ready, steady...

Pffft, pffft...

Oh rats.

Try as he might, he couldn't whistle. Mort had never been able to whistle. Why hadn't he thought of that before?

Wait!

Mort grabbed a raven between his hands and gently squeezed it until the bird peeped in alarm. He squeezed two more times, until he had the complete call:

PEEP ... PEEP ... PURP

(close enough)

The pigeon stopped in its tracks and turned round. Sensing the significance of the moment, the ravens cleared a path for it and the pigeon waddled slowly towards Mort and held up its scaly leg for him to inspect.

The whole thing was a bit strange but Mort didn't want to be rude so he took the pigeon's leg in his fingers and looked closely at the red tag attached to it. Inside it was a scroll of paper and a pencil! He could send a message!

Mort quickly began to write...

After squeezing another raven three times, Mort sent the strange pigeon winging its way back to Dead Man's Island, with words for Ono attached to its scaly leg.

A few hours later, Plop Assunder's little boat was bucking on the waves like a truly awful fairground ride and Mort was trying not to be sick. But he was, constantly. Ono was at the helm, steering and singing a sea shanty she'd made up.

"Here comes a wave,
And here comes another.
We'll live through the storms
If we cling to each other..."

It would be nice to say that Ono's voice soothed Mort's turbulent mind and stomach, but for the entire journey he had his head over the side of the boat and his fingers firmly in his ears. He didn't even hear Ono's gleeful shout of, "We're home!" as Dead Man's Island popped into view.

As they neared the north side, Mort's face was still in the water. He didn't miss much – just a wet, black, shiny cliff face dripping with the ocean's spew. It was so ominous and foreboding that anyone passing would think it was a perilous place to land. But Dead Man's Island was like a slice of sponge cake sinking lopsidedly into a custard pond, and round the back it was a completely different kettle of fish. From the south side, the island was a sloping tabletop of verdant green, carved into giant steps that held fields for flowers, huts for shelter, bars for sailors.

You heard.

When Mort finally lifted his head out of the sea, with a small squid clinging to his fringe, it was this – the paradise side – that he saw.

"Welcome to Dead Man's Island!" Ono said, laughing at the shock on Mort's face.

WHOOOOAAAAAA!

Mort's mouth dropped open, releasing a rush of surprise and a small hermit crab.

He had never seen such a carnival of colour. The flowers! Ono had been right – the marigolds were enormous and incredible sunflowers stretched towards the sky with heads as big as saucepans (*really* big ones). The whole place was bursting and popping with brilliant colour and abundance.

"How come your flowers grow bigger than mine?"

"Dead men," Ono said, winking.

Let that sink in a bit.

A little longer.

There.

When they docked, Ono took Mort straight to the Waterfall of Loveliness (which thundered with fresh, drinkable water), and they washed the sea from their hair and clothes. Mort discovered that Ono's grey, salty hair was grey even when it wasn't salty, making her even more interesting, Mort thought.

Ono Assunder was like a miracle friend – she was easy-going and happy; she spoke of good things and then made them appear. Like the forests and plantations on Dead Man's Island, bursting with exotic fruits – enough to make health-boosting smoothies for all of Brutalia.

"How Mags would have loved this!" Mort sighed.

"Mags the Witch?" Ono asked.

"Yes, but she wasn't a witch."

"She probably was, you know, but if it makes you feel any better she does love it here."

Ono pointed to a palm tree that fanned above them, filled with little fruits and pretty parrots.

"She's in the tree?"

"Well, she's under it." Ono shrugged.

Mort gently stroked the trunk of the tree and he smiled. Even horrible endings had new beginnings here, on this island of perfection. And, up until this point, Mort had almost forgotten that beneath their feet were dead people.

Then out of nowhere came a haunting noise.

Mort froze. "What's that?"

There were voices, swelling and fading, swelling and fading, like a ghostly symphony on the wind. He gripped Ono's arm.

"I hear dead people," he shuddered.

"Do you?" she said, surprised.

"Listen to that sound. It's the sigh of dead men..." he said, teeth chattering.

Ono stood still and listened. "Oh, that! Nah, that's

just the sailors. Come on, let's go and meet them."

These were the very same sailors the ravens would so love to pluck to pieces. And, if they'd been shipwrecked on Brutalia, the birds would have plucked away. But for some time the sailors' ships had been coming across mysterious signs bobbing in the water, advertising Paradise Cocktails and Clean Sheets. And they all pointed in the direction of Dead Man's Island. For a weary sailor in search of a cocktail bar and a bug-free bed, it was a no-brainer.

(It was a no-brainer for the ravens too, seeing as it meant no more sailor brains got served up on Brutalia's spiky coastline.)

Mort and Ono stopped at a large shack. The song Mort heard wasn't haunting at all, but jolly, loud and clear, and had something to do with rum and finding love on the ocean waves. There was a sign outside the shack that read:

Welcome
To
The
LAND LUBBERS
Bar
LEAVE YOUR SEA PETS
AND SEA LEGS
AT THE DOOR

Tied outside were temporary-pet octopuses (temporary because they were slippery little suckers and always escaped), and leaning up against the walls were a few wooden legs and arms.

"Come on, they're inside," Ono said.

"Who *are* they?"

"Passing sailors. They come and drink our pawpaw juice and eat our food and give us money and interesting trinkets in return. It's a pretty good arrangement."

"What happened to their legs and arms?"

"Sea monsters took them," Ono said, shaking her head. "The sailors are always daring each other to fight creatures of the deep and it's not always a clean fight. Come on, I'll introduce you to Priscilla. She arm-wrestled a great white shark. Believe it or not, the shark lost. That's her leg there."

"Why aren't they allowed to wear their wooden arms and legs?"

"We ask them to leave them outside because it gets a bit rowdy in there," Ono explained. "They tend to swing them about a lot and it can lead to accidents."

While an octopus slipped its collar and headed back to the sea, Mort and Ono ventured into the Landlubbers Bar. Sailors with flushed, merry cheeks were singing and swaying and knocking together glasses of brightly coloured fruit drinks. Mort and Ono were immediately caught up in the push and pull of the party, suffocating in the armpits of sailors who were swigging pawpaw juice above their heads.

Ono grabbed Mort's arm. "Oh dear, they're nearly at the chorus. Unless you want to get caught up in repeating the same line over and over all evening, we should go. Come on, I'll take you to the beach and you can tell me all about your problems."

They both gulped in the fresh air on the other side of the bar door as the sailors began hitting the high notes.

"How did you know I have problems?" Mort panted.

Ono unrolled the piece of paper Mort had attached to the pigeon.

Come and get me or I'm a dead man.

"Oh yeah. That."

In his wonderment at Dead Man's Island, Mort had almost forgotten his plea for help. Because he didn't need it any more. He'd arrived in paradise.

"You'll let me stay here, won't you?"

"Of course. But it's not just because we grow better flowers, is it? Tell me why you want to stay."

"It's because I'm gutless," Mort said. "I'm running away."

Ono and Mort sat silently, toes burrowing into the fine golden sand, blinking at the sun's sparkles on the water. The warm breeze flipped their hair as the sea washed up and down the beach.

"There, we've done the dramatic pause bit," Ono said. "Now spill the beans."

So Mort told Ono all about it – from start to finish – and he thought he'd made the whole story clear.

"You mean you're saving your friend Weed from a date with death by killing him in less than three days' time, but your plan is now in danger because, despite defeating Warren the tiger, tomorrow you're almost certainly going to die at the paws of a Grot Bear?"

"Yes."

"Well, I think running away is quite a sensible thing to do in that case," Ono said.

"That saves me but it doesn't save Weed, does it? And this whole story is about me saving Weed. Do you think I need to be the main character in a different story – one where there's no death?"

Ono said nothing, and Mort thought momentarily about swimming out into the sunset sea and forgetting all about it. But Weed... Those chocolatey eyes that had smiled at his jokes, widened with delight as they ate forbidden doughnuts and gone gooey when Mort had told him he was his best friend ever... He couldn't abandon him. He just couldn't.

"You're stuck," Ono said. "But if Weed is going to get the chop anyway nothing you do will save him. If you run away, at least you'll avoid a fight with a Grot Bear. And fighting anything is not my idea of fun. I'm a pacifist, you see."

NO WAY!

"No way! So am I!" Mort said. "I'm a pacifist too. A proper one."

Ono coughed. "Wait a minute. You say you're a pacifist, but you're the Royal Executioner. *You're Mort the Brute.*"

The words were like spears of ice piercing Mort's warm happiness.

"It wasn't my choice. I don't want to kill anyone. I never asked to be brutal."

"Are you sure?" Ono enquired seriously.

Mort nodded.

"So there are two of us pacifists? This is the best news ever!"

"Certainly is," Mort said. "We should join forces. Without any force, of course."

They high-fived and danced in the sand before getting distracted by a stranded jellyfish, which they helped back into the water. Then they hugged because they were both caring and brilliant people. And then they sat and watched the sun set.

It was perfect.

Although... Mort's mind was suddenly struck by the image of Weed Millet, shivering in fear in a puddle of rat wee at the back of a dark dungeon.

"What's the matter, Mort?" Ono said, skimming a seashell across the glistening water.

"I'm worried I might be more gutless than pacifist,"

Mort said. "It's a deep and meaningful conversation I keep having with myself."

Ono put her arm round Mort's shoulders. "I find that, when I have a problem, it's best to sleep on it. Come on, let's go back to the Landlubbers Bar and get you a nice drink of pawpaw. Then you can stay in the guest house for the night. It's a perfect place for sleeping on a problem. I can promise you, this will be a night's sleep like you've never had before."

CHAPTER TEN
GUTS

"What sort of food do you think there is in paradise?"

"I don't know, but I think there's plenty to drink."

"Why's that?"

"Paradise always starts with a pee."

"I wish I hadn't asked..."

The tinkle of birdsong filtered through the curtains and a gentle breeze brushed Mort's cheeks. His eyes flickered. He sat up, fresh from the best night's sleep he'd ever had.

I'm in heaven, Mort thought, blinking a thousand times.

Indeed, what he'd seen on Dead Man's Island had momentarily tricked Mort into thinking life was perfect. That nothing could go wrong.

(If you're a fan of pantomimes, feel free to shout:

Oh yes it could!)

Mort looked round his beautiful guest room, decorated with exotic blooms and fruit platters. Ono had thought of everything – there was even a cuddly chinchilla at the bottom of his bed.

Mort never wanted to leave such a wonderful place. But you can't stay in bed playing with a chinchilla all day, can you? (What's that? Oh sorry, apparently you *can* stay in bed playing with a chinchilla all day.)

Luckily Mort *didn't* spend a long time in bed playing with a chinchilla, because, if he had done, there wouldn't have been time to have a heroic moment, which was crucial to getting this story back on track.

Mort stepped outside into a flower garden. It was alive with butterflies and dragonflies. In Brutalia there were fruit flies, and cockroaches, and ants, and... No, that's it – fruit flies, cockroaches and ants. If Gosh and Gee could only see this!

Gosh and Gee. He hadn't thought about those lovable, scrappy ratbags in a while. Were they OK? Had they lost more teeth? Did they miss him?

Mort was suddenly struck by a **strange feeling** (a bit like being seasick).

It vanished when a parrot with red-and-gold wings flew past. Filled with awe, he followed it to the edge of the land and looked out across the waves. The sea here was blue, not grey like the waters that surrounded Brutalia, and it was choppy only because of the dolphins that were tumbling through it. In the distance a white ship bobbed closer, heading for the south beach, bringing sailors, songs and trinkets.

This was a dreamland.

Mort pinched himself, which was just about OK according to the Pacifist Code.

And his mother – oh, if his mother could see this! Mort reckoned such beautiful views would soothe her soul and she'd never pick up a set of battle cutlery again.

Then came that **strange feeling** again (like when you're up a ladder and scared of heights).

What was that **strange feeling** (like when you speed over a bump in the car)?

"How are you feeling?" Ono said at his shoulder.

"I was just trying to work that out."

"I have to get another body with Dad – someone choked on a rat – but do make yourself at home. After all, this is your home now. I'll see you later!"

Mort watched Ono disappear over the hill. Wonderful Ono, with her funny name and grey hair and cloudy eyes, was the most amazing new friend... Then Mort remembered his amazing *old* friend, rotting in a cell with two days to live.

He was filled with a **strange feeling**...

Weed, oh, Weed. Our last words were so unsatisfactory, Mort thought. *Wait, what were our last words?*

(Hang on a minute... Just looking, just looking. Ah, here they are.)

"Do me a favour. Tell my parents to stop baking. If the King and Queen find out they've baked more than their rationed amount, they'll end up in here with me."

Oh no! In trying to save his own life, Mort had not kept his one simple promise. Now they were all in danger.

The **strange feeling** churned again like—

"This has gone on WAY too long," Mort said to the chinchilla on his shoulder. "It doesn't matter if this **strange feeling** doesn't have a label, like sadness or guilt or worry or whatever. I know it's trying to tell me something."

It was trying to tell him lots of things actually. Like how home wasn't a place but the people in it, and how friendship, love and loyalty might be a bit more important than soft pillows and chinchilla hugs. But the **strange feeling** he was experiencing was more than homesickness...

Ultimately it was uncomfortable being gutless.

Well, it would be, wouldn't it? Having no guts

would leave you with an empty space inside – a space that would show up on an X-ray. That's bound to feel a bit strange.

"This is paradise," Mort declared. "But I can't stay, knowing that I ran away and left the people I love in danger. I might be Mort the Meek, but I'm not Mort the Mean."

Ono was down at the busy harbour, about to push the boat off. Plop was already aboard. They looked up at the sound of Mort's heroic-sounding footsteps.

"Wait, wait!" Mort cried. "I'm not gutless – I'm not!"

"What are you then?" Ono said, steadying the boat.

"I don't know!"

"OK," said Ono patiently. "Let's work through this. If you're not gutless, then you're what? Gutty, gutful, guttural...?"

"I think it's just that **I've got guts**, meaning I'm not afraid to face my responsibilities."

"Great, that's sorted. Enjoy your guts!"

"But ... how can I face my responsibilities and fight when I'm a pacifist? Oh look, a pretty fish!" Mort pointed at the harbour waters, which were teeming with fish all colours of the rainbow.

"That's it!" Ono cried.

"Slap them with pretty fish?" Mort gasped.

"You know, you're sounding a bit silly now," Ono sighed. "What I meant was **we need a distraction**."

"Yes, Ono. What a brilliant idea. We need to distract the Grot Bear!" Mort's excited face fell suddenly, like Mrs Millet into a pile of dough. "In just a few hours' time the Queen wants to see me fight... I don't think distraction will be enough."

Speaking of distractions, Ono and Mort were interrupted by a cackle of laughter from one of the ships, where two seafarers called Duncan and Priscilla were making really bad jokes as they waited for their ship to set sail.

"Why wasn't the sailor allowed in the Landlubbers Bar? Because he was already legless!" Priscilla laughed, knocking on her wooden leg.

"And why was the captain angry? Because the sailor only gave him one aye," snorted Duncan, popping out his glass eye.

They were joined by a sailor who gave them a hand with their jokes. And another who wanted to lend an ear.

Ono and Mort turned to each other slowly and nodded, because how cool is it to have exactly the same genius idea at exactly the same time?

Very.

CHAPTER ELEVEN
THE GROTESQUE FIGHT

"Are you a lover or a fighter, do you think?"

"Definitely a lover."

"What if I told you I'd just spotted an eyeball?"

"I'd fight you for it."

They say that beauty is in the eye of the beholder but the Grot Bear was ugly no matter how you looked at it. It was foaming at the mouth and its back was broad and as knobbly as a knuckle stick.

Mort stood calmly as the beast, still chained at a safe distance, grasped at imaginary flies in front of its face.

"Hey, you," Mort said, thinking it was important to show the Queen he had the upper hand.

The beast looked at him and did a weird lizardy-tongue-lick thing. Only the Grot Bear's tongue wasn't thin and wispy – it was like a slab of meat.

What sort of Grot Bear is it? Is it a lover or a fighter?

Mort was just asking himself questions to pass the time, because the answer didn't matter. The ones who were lovers crushed you with love, and the ones who weren't crushed you for the hell of it. The outcome always involved getting crushed, which was pretty ugly however you looked at it.

"Are you ready?" Malc Clam roared with evident pleasure.

"I am!" the Queen declared, wriggling on her child-seat. Malc was actually talking to Mort, but didn't dare correct her.

"Wonderful, Your Majesties. Shall we begin?"

The people of Brutalia were, once again, not invited, but the King was present, having managed to leave his bedroom that morning, only his child-chair had collapsed and he was now on the floor, unable to get back up.

There was a hollow clanging of metal as the chains and shackles were stripped from the Grot Bear.

Unaccustomed to freedom, it shook itself all over like a dog and then bit its tongue – **OW!** It stopped to stroke the wounded slab of meat in its mouth and that's when Mort knew that this one was a love-crusher. That made him feel bad. But it also made him feel good. He had a plan in place for love-crushers – a plan that meant he might just be able to keep to his pacifist principles.

"Oi! Cuddle monster, over here!" Mort taunted.

The Grot Bear looked up. Its eyebrows bunched together as its eyes worked out what the shape in front of it was. A human child. A child! A baby person! So cute... CUDDLE!

The Grot Bear lumbered forward with its arms open wide and Mort shouted:

"I AM MORT THE BRUTE!"

(Which is what the royals were expecting.)

The Queen cheered. (Little did she know it was a signal.)

Seemingly from out of nowhere, a swarm of sailors entered the square (followed by some hopeful ravens). They were waving swords and funny hand-held things that went

BANG! BANG! BANG! BANG!

It startled the Queen, the King, the Grot and the Clam. Even the ravens stopped for a moment. But Mort was startle-free. He knew exactly what was about to happen. But let's get back to the *BANG-BANG-BANGS...*

The cowardly King shuffled painfully on his bottom out of the square to safety. The Queen remained, transfixed by the goings-on.

Brutalia had never had visitors before. Foreign

boats, which always crashed into the rocky north side of the island, quickly sank and their sailors became raven food. And as for other adventurers who might wish to set foot on this cruel rock – well, that's the thing: not one of them ever did. Why would they want to? Brutalia had no wealth and no decent bars. It offered nothing but cruelty and brutalism, and life was already short enough without bothering with all that.

"Don't worry, Your Majesty," Mort said, keeping an eye on the approaching Grot Bear. "I'll deal with them."

The Queen almost looked grateful.

The sailors stormed the stage, knocking the Grot Bear right off it and into a cart of dough. (It had been wheeled there as part of this most ingenious plan.)

"Get him, lads and Priscilla!" a big sailor bellowed, pointing at Mort.

"I'm not scared of you!" Mort bellowed back.

The sailors formed an orderly queue in front of Mort, just as they'd arranged, and then began their fight sequence. They hadn't had long to practise, but it was pretty easy to get the hang of.

Fight Sequence:

Mort grabbed the first
sailor and ripped off her leg.
"Ow!" said Priscilla,
who winked and then
picked it up and hopped
away.

Mort plucked an eyeball
from the next sailor in line.

Then an ear from another.

And a hand from the next.
A nose from—

"Hair," the sailor growled, through gritted teeth. *"I'm the one with a wig."*

"Sorry," said Mort, releasing his nose. Mort tore the wig from his scalp.

Then came the sailor with the stick-on nose.

"Now leave Brutalia and don't ever come back!" shouted Mort.

"You're way too scary for us," the sailors said. "We're running away and we'll never come back!"

The Queen, who had turned a strange shade of yellow in alarm, began to turn pink again. She clapped her hands.

"Bravo, Mort the Brute! I had no idea these revolting sailors had even landed on my shores.

But you dispatched them with such brilliance. It was a masterclass in brutality."

She turned to Malc Clam. "Satisfied?"

Malc nodded and did that apologetic bowing thing, but it wasn't enough.

"You've wasted everybody's time, Mr Clam. Off to the tower with you!" The Queen clicked her fingers, but no other guards were there so she took him herself.

"And Mort," came her irritating voice from far away, "I'm looking forward to that execution…"

Mort scrambled down to the shoreline, where his friend and the sailors were waiting to say goodbye.

"You did it!" Ono said quietly, patting Mort on the back. "You showed you were a brutalist without being brutal at all! I have to say, it looked pretty grotty from where I was standing. Especially Duncan's eyeball."

Grotty… Where was the Grot Bear?

The Grot Bear was still in the cart, fast asleep and sunk deep into the soft, squidgy dough, cuddling it as hard as it could. *Aw...*

It was as if everything had come together in perfect harmony. The Millets' house was now half emptied of dough, the Grot Bear was happily crushing something that couldn't die and the Queen was certain Mort was a brutalist. There was nothing left to do.

Almost nothing left to do...

The Queen's final words swam round and round and round like a whirlpool of doom.

And she didn't have to wait long. The brutalist display – or reckoning or knuckling or whatever – was in two days. Doesn't time go fast when you're watching other people struggle with a difficult plot!

"Back to Dead Man's Island for a well-earned pawpaw juice! Last one there's a rotten mollusc!" The sailors cheered. They clambered aboard their ship with an *oh-ho-ho*, taking the Grot Bear in the dough cart with them (they needed a new pet since their octopuses had fled).

"*Are you coming?*" Ono whispered.

"I've got to sort out some things here." Mort smiled. "Maybe later."

"If you need me, I'm only a pigeon away," Ono said. "I've got to go now – got to help Dad with a body. Some old man at number fifty-four Pitch Street."

Mort's heart stopped still.

"Dad...?"

"No, wait, it's number **sixty**-four Pitch Street. My bad."

Mort clutched his chest as his heart thudded painfully back to life.

"Bye, Ono."

"Bye, Mort."

Mort sat in the square. The surge of elation he'd felt on getting past the problem of the Grot Bear had disappeared gently but quickly, like a mug of perfect hot chocolate. Only it didn't leave him warm and happy and it didn't come with a marshmallow on the side.

Mort had faced challenge after challenge. But the worst was yet to come.

Weed.

Weed, oh, Weed. Our last words were so unsatisfactory, Mort thought again.

Wait! Weed's final words... Had Mort remembered them correctly? No! After the bit about the baking, Weed had said something else.

"And, if you want a sense of purpose, why don't you think about not killing me a bit more?"

Those were Weed's final words. Why hadn't he thought about not killing him a bit more? Mort, in his gutless phase, had pushed it out of his mind altogether.

(Science bit: he hadn't *really* pushed it out of his mind altogether – the information he was now remembering had been safely stored in the part of the brain responsible for memory. And, quite by chance, also some of the ravens' food of choice.)

Mort was no longer in his gutless phase.

He wasn't Mort the Meek or Mort the Brute or Mort the Mean.

He was in his

Mort the Mighty phase!

He thought briefly about asking his mum to sew a Mort the Mighty badge on to his pyjamas. But, before he designed it, he had to earn it.

He had to be Mighty. And he had to be Mighty mighty quickly.

CHAPTER TWELVE
BRAIN OVER BRAWN

"We need to think about this intelligently."

"Thinking too much fries my brain."

*"That's it! If we could get the people of Brutalia
to think, maybe they'd fry their brains!"*

"Come on, Brutalia ...
THINK! THINK! THINK!"

The next day Mort woke full of determination, and immediately looked around him for inspiration as to how not to kill his best friend. But there was no bolt of brilliance or gong-bashing brainwave. Brutalia's misery clouded his mind and blanked out his creativity, and he could only ask himself a series of strange questions followed by even stranger answers. Like this:

What had Brutalia ever done for anyone?
NOTHING!
Well, it did provide a tiny damp space to call your own.

Apart from providing people with a tiny damp space to call their own, what had Brutalia ever done for anyone?
NOTHING!
It provided entertainment, if you liked that sort of thing.

Apart from providing people with a tiny damp space to call their own, and entertainment, if you liked that sort of thing, what had Brutalia ever done for anyone?
NOTHING!
It taught people how to fight.

ALL RIGHT. *Apart from providing people with a tiny damp space to call their own, and entertainment, if you liked that sort of thing, and teaching people to fight ... what had Brutalia ever done for anyone?*

Er... **NOTHING.**

Mort's strange conversation with himself about Brutalia left him so miserable he was ready to chop his own head off. It was as if his get-up-and-go had taken a quick look around and got-up-and-gone. It was all very well puffing out your chest like an overstuffed pillow, and calling yourself Mort the Mighty, but what use was it if you didn't have a plan?

No genius strategy had struck like it had on the beautiful shores of Dead Man's Island and Mort realized why. It was because Dead Man's Island was the multicoloured land of the free – it let your mind soar. Brutalia was nothing but a cruel master that extracted life, love and hope like a terrible dentist extracts teeth with no painkillers. Its ominous towers stood in the way of creative thinking and its fearful grip stopped you from exploring new possibilities. It made everything black and white, like the island's rubbish motto:

LIVE OR DIE

Without a plan, Weed was still on a set path to **DIE**. Which was disappointing.

Worse than that, he was on a set path to **DIE** believing that his best friend didn't care. Which was *really* sad.

Mort did care – and he had to tell Weed right away that he was thinking more about not killing him. Although he hadn't come up with an escape plan, he was working on it, and that was a really good start...

He remembered seeing something that boosted brainpower in FORAGING FOR NATURE STUFF. He'd stumbled upon an interesting rhyme that might help.

> *For mental focus*
> *Pick not a crocus*
> *Nor a plant with floral print.*
> *Pick rosemary and sage*
> *(Drawn on the next page)*
> *With leaves of fresh peppermint.*
> *And basil.*

Mort did as the little book advised and swigged a leafy tea, fragrant with focus-boosting herbs. Then he headed to Brutalia's depressing prison, stopping first at the Millets' for a bag of doughnuts for Brutus, the prison guard. Despite his warning, the Millets had begun excessively baking again, which Mort could *really, really, really* have done without. But he'd worry about that later.

"Weed?"

"I'm not talking to you," said a pathetic voice in the darkness.

"I understand, but I'm going to talk to you whether you like it or not. I've been thinking more about not killing you, Weed."

There was a clinking and rattling as Weed stirred in the darkness. "You have? You're saving my life?"

"At some point. Maybe. Er, let's go for a walk. I've had a chat with Brutus and he's going to unchain you, aren't you, Brutus?"

There was a slight delay as the giant guard struggled

to get through the cell door to unshackle Weed. It was all pretty awkward.

"Come on then, you snivelling, grovelling, raven-stealing goat fart!" Mort said in his most brutish voice.

"What?" Weed said before he remembered. "Oh yeah, that's me."

"I'm going to take you out of here and parade you round the town and you're going to see just what you'll be missing when you're dead in one day's time! Ha ha ha ha!"

"You're sounding very brutal, Mort the Brute," the Every-ten-minute Horn Blower said with admiration. Then he did his thing with the horn and disappeared again.

"Right, ready to go?" Mort said, helping Weed down the tunnel.

"This is it! We're escaping, aren't we?" Weed said hopefully. "You really *have* thought of something, haven't you?"

Mort didn't want to lie so said nothing.

He was thinking hard, he really was. And Mags's potion was definitely taking effect. Mort hadn't thought of a plan yet but he had come up with a better idea for a Mort the Mighty badge. Even though he hadn't earned it yet. Which was a bit naughty.

"You'll pay for this," came a voice from another cell. It was Malc Clam – who didn't look quite so threatening, standing in his pants with a rat on his head. "Mort the Meek, I'll see that you die a horrible, slow and painful death, just like your friend."

"Spit at him, Mort," Weed said. "Tell Brutus to chop off his fingers."

Mort stood close to the bars, but he didn't spit. He just thought how having a name that spelled the same forwards and backwards didn't help in any way when you were in Brutalia's dank dark prison. He reached into his pocket where he'd placed a couple of emergency doughnuts and pulled them out.

"Eat one in front of him," Weed said.

Instead Mort pushed the doughnut through the bars. It was a messy job.

He and Weed walked away to the sound of Malc

gobbling the sugary treat.

Outside the prison Weed blinked lots, roughly a million times. There wasn't sunlight as such in Brutalia but it was bright compared with the dungeons where Weed had sat for six days in complete darkness.

"I'm free! Free! *Freeeeee!*" he sang.

"Stop shouting," Mort pleaded.

"Who wouldn't shout at being *freeeeee!*"

Mort's idea to let Weed get a bit of fresh air was backfiring.

Why had he given Weed this false sense of freedom – or trusted Mags's potion to give him the brainpower he needed? All his brain was telling him was that no, they couldn't make an escape, even if it did look like the perfect opportunity. And here's why.

Why couldn't they run?

Because the Queen wanted a show.

Couldn't they just sail away and forget all about the Queen?

Where would they sail to?

What if they sailed to Dead Man's Island?

If the Queen sent out a search party and found the

island, Mort would be putting everyone's life there at
risk.

**Couldn't the sailors fight and protect Dead
Man's Island?**

*Maybe, but most of the time they were drunk on
pawpaw juice and, even if they weren't, the island would
be found and things would never be the same again.*

**Couldn't they cross that bridge when they
came to it?**

*No, and look, these questions are starting to get just a
teensy-weensy bit irritating, so, if you don't mind, please
read the following sentence and then stop with all the
questions, OK?*

**At the end of the day, the Queen wanted to
see a body.**

Wanted to see a body.

Wanted to see a body.

Wanted to see a body.

Wanted to see a body.

Wanted to see a body.

What a strange and haunting echo! Mort looked around, but could see nobody there. That was weird.

"So where are we going, Mort?" Weed said, tugging his sleeve.

"Don't worry about where we're going. There are people watching us. Just look as if you're about to die."

Weed already looked as if he was about to die. His hair was greasy and his once wonderful chocolatey eyes were now hollow in his pale, pale face, like thumbprints in a dough ball.

Like thumbprints in a dough ball.

Like thumbprints in a dough ball.

Like thumbprints in a dough ball.

Like thumbprints in a dough ball.

Like thumbprints in a dough ball.

Like thumbprints in a dough ball.

Another strange and haunting echo! Mort looked around, but could see nobody there. That was weird.

"Are you all right?" Weed asked Mort, who had stopped abruptly and was scratching his head.

"Yeah... I just keep hearing things," Mort said.

"Well, I didn't say anything," Weed said. "I'm pretending to be nearly dead. And nearly dead people don't speak."

Pretending to be nearly dead.

Pretending to be nearly dead.

Pretending to be nearly dead.

Pretending to be nearly dead.

Pretending to be nearly dead.

Pretending to be nearly dead.

"Keep going," Mort said, his step quickening. "I think I'm about to come up with a great idea."

"I thought you'd already had one."

"No, I was lying. But don't worry, a plan is forming. I just need two more pieces of the puzzle and then I can work it out."

"Can we pop in and see Mum and Dad?" Weed said. "They'll be worrying about me."

"Yes, they will ... and I hate to break it to you, but they're still baking mad."

Baking mad.

Baking mad.

Baking mad.

Baking mad.

Baking mad.

Baking mad.

"Mort, are you feeling OK?"

"Yes, Weed, yes I am. Because, if I'm not mistaken, I just picked up another piece of the puzzle. Come on, let's go!"

Mort dragged his friend away from the main streets and into the slithery side streets and bilious backstreets of Brutalia. The boy stumbled and tripped. Passers-by stared at Weed's pathetic figure and shivered, as if they were looking at a dead boy walking. Mort thought he should collect flowers and herbs to build up Weed's strength, which was waning.

A flock of ravens, now scrawny from hunger, followed closely. They wanted to be the first on the scene to check for signs of life when Weed finally collapsed. With any luck there wouldn't be any.

"Argh!"

"What is it, Weed?" Mort said, dragging his fallen friend up from the muddy ground.

"They're after me. The ravens – they're after me for what I did."

"You didn't do anything, Weed. It was the raven's fault it got caught in your net."

"Maybe it wasn't. Maybe I meant to catch it. Because who ever heard of a raven eating loganberries?"

"Listen to me. It is *not your fault*. These ravens are so hungry they'll eat anything. Anything!"

These ravens are so hungry they'll eat anything. Anything!

These ravens are so hungry they'll eat anything. Anything!

These ravens are so hungry they'll eat anything. Anything!

These ravens are so hungry they'll eat anything. Anything!

These ravens are so hungry they'll eat anything. Anything!

These ravens are so hungry they'll eat anything. Anything!

"BINGO!"

CHAPTER THIRTEEN

A SHORT CHAPTER ABOUT A PUZZLE

"I've got an idea."

"Can I have some of your eye, dear?"

"What? No! I said an IDEA."

"What is it?"

"I've forgotten it now."

With less than twenty-four hours before Weed's execution, let's quickly run through what happened immediately after Mort said **"BINGO!"**

Weed asked what BINGO meant and Mort admitted he didn't know, but it sounded good. So they shouted it together for fun.

Mort took Weed back to prison, which Weed wasn't expecting. Being a brutalist (and not a pacifist), he tried to punch Mort. Mort was a little hurt (emotionally) but could understand why Weed would do it (he was very understanding). But he had no choice because the Queen needed a body.

Mort visited Malc's cell with a big bag of doughnuts.

Mort found the pigeon with the red tag and sent it off with three peeps of a squeezed raven back to Dead Man's Island.

Then Mort went to solve a puzzle. He needed silence, focus and concentration. So he probably shouldn't have gone home to do it.

"Mort's back! Yay!"

Oh, how wonderful it was to see their little faces! He was going to hug them tight and tell them about an island so beautiful it would bring peace to their hearts.

"Yes, I'm back. Shall I tell you a story about a magical island?" Mort said.

"No. Let's fight!"

"No fighting, please," Mort pleaded.

Gosh and Gee high-fived each other and then ran at him head first, intending to ram him in the stomach. Their heads bashed into each other before they even reached him, and they knocked each other unconscious and fell to the floor.

Mort scooped them up and placed them in their beds with slices of cold turnip on their heads. He looked at the green-and-blue bruises on their angelic faces and silently promised them that one day he'd invent toys so they wouldn't have to beat each other up for fun.

But, for now, he had a puzzle to do.

As he was about to start, the door slammed and his mum stood in front of him, eyes flaring and wild. "Mort! The next-door neighbour called me a stinky sausage, and your dad's not here to defend my honour. I've got the forks ready. Grab a couple of plates and meet me over there."

"No, Mum," Mort said firmly.

"What you do you mean – no?" she said.

"Why don't you just ignore them?" Mort suggested. "You know you're not a stinky sausage, so who cares what they say? Don't worry about your honour. Defend your dignity."

Mort's mum considered his wise words a while. "Nah, I'm gonna chuck forks at 'em," she said and disappeared.

You can't win 'em all. Mort sighed.

Now, back to his puzzle.

"Mort..."

What now?

"Dad, I thought you were out. Mum's next door fighting the neighbours. They called her a stinky sausage."

"Yeah, well, that pub landlady – Publinka Dunker – called me a frog's bum. I said you'd sort her out. Come on."

"Seriously?" Mort said. "You want me to sentence Publinka Dunker to death because she called you a frog's bum?"

"Of course. You're Mort the Brute. What use are you if you can't kill someone for calling your old dad a frog's bum?"

"May I remind you, Dad, that last week you called Mum a *pooey loo brush*, you told Gosh and Gee they were *herring snot* and you said I looked like a *slug that had just eaten a slug...* If you want to go down that route, I'm happy to take you before the Queen and King. Shall we go?"

Mort's dad tapped his chin. "Forget it, son. It's nothing."

Finally Mort could get back to his puzzle. He got all the pieces out of his mind pouch, and moved them around and around and around and around...

These ravens are so hungry they'll eat anything. **Anything!**

Pretending to be nearly dead

?

LIKE THUMBPRINTS IN A DOUGH BALL...

Baking mad!

WANTED TO SEE A BODY...

It was shaping up nicely, but Mort needed a final bolt of brilliance.

"Think, Mort!" Mort instructed himself.

"Think about what?" Mort asked himself grumpily.

"Think about things in a different way."

"YOU try thinking about things in a different way if you know everything."

"All right, I will."

Mort lay down and closed his eyes and pictured himself on Dead Man's Island, where nothing was black and white and anything was possible.

CHAPTER FOURTEEN
THE STAGE IS SET

"Chop Chop!"

"I'm flying as fast as I can."

*"Chop Chop. It's the name of the restaurant
we're going to. The food is fresh and
the execution is excellent!"*

"Oh, I get it. Very funny. Bagsy the eyeballs."

In Brutalia's square the atmosphere was electric and jumpy (and not just because the guards were prodding the crowd with sticks).

From where the Queen and King were sitting, it looked as if the whole of Brutalia was excitedly awaiting the execution. A few fights were breaking out, which was making the Grot Bears nervous – especially the cuddly ones – and all of it pleased the Queen immensely, as today she was feeling nasty. Nastier than nasty. **Nastionormous.**

This was because the King had not only belched and farted throughout their Royal Wedding Anniversary Breakfast, he'd also tried to kiss her, and she was definitely **NOT** in the mood for that. What she was in the mood for was a really good brutalist display. And she was ready for it **now**.

She nodded her head at Hulk Poodle, a man with a chiselled jaw and startlingly good hair. Hulk had replaced poor Malc Clam as the Queen's personal bodyguard. She'd chosen him herself.

Hulk raised his arms in the air and up went signs on sticks saying *CHEER NOW*.

The people cheered for the Queen. The people cheered because 'special-occasion carrots' were being thrown. (Fresh, blemish-free carrots were often thrown at big events to create fights as people scrambled for them.)

From outside the prison Mort could hear it all. And it chilled him to the core.

Most of the cheers would be forced out of people with electric prods, plenty of *CHEER NOW* signs and free, blemish-free vegetables; he'd been to enough events to know that. But many Brutalians were raised brutal and he knew that, among them, some might even be looking forward to seeing the death of his best friend, a boy aged only twelve, although he looked thirteen and a half.

How could people be like that – so savage and cruel? The thought made Mort feel sick. But he swallowed it back down. He couldn't afford to be ill now – Weed was depending on him. And he didn't have FORAGING FOR NATURE STUFF to hand. That was full of vomit remedies.

The prison gates wheezed open and Brutus emerged

with the doomed prisoner. Weed was on the end of a long chain fixed round his wrists; his shaking made the chain rattle, like a rattle of doom. Not like a rattle of doom – it **was** a rattle of doom because, as far as Weed knew, this was it. He was going to die.

And his ~~best friend~~ ex-best friend and cruel betrayer was going to kill him.

Mort passed Brutus a bumper bag of doughnuts and leaned forward menacingly.

"Two things," Mort said with a snarl he'd been practising. "Release everyone in the prison. The Queen wants them to watch the execution and shake in fear. And you'd better believe me or there won't be any more doughnuts."

"Yeah, all right. What's the other thing?"

"Give me Weed Millet. I will take him to the square myself."

It wasn't usual for the executioner to collect the prisoner. If you remember, Bob the Brute liked everyone to be there before him so he could make his 'dramatic entrance'.

But this execution was going to be different.

So very different.

Even more different than you're imagining.

No, more than that.

You're not even close.

Mort released Weed and began to lead him towards the square, where the cheers had turned to screams because a Grot Bear had got loose.

Mort dragged Weed down a stinking side alley and, when he was sure they were alone, he retrieved a small glass bottle from his coat.

"*Drink this quickly, for strength,*" he whispered.

"Brutus told me you were going to kill me horribly. Poison, is it? A slow, painful death in one of Brutalia's barfing backstreets. No thanks."

"*You have to trust me,*" Mort hissed.

"But you locked me back up. How can I trust you after that?"

"Because what's your other option?"

As far as Weed could work out, the choice was death or death.

Death or death was no choice at all, so really he had nothing to lose. And, on the chance it might not turn

out to be death, Weed grabbed the bottle from Mort.
He threw the contents down his throat and fell to his
knees. He raised his face to the sky and closed his eyes.

"Take me, death. Take me, for I am ready. Take
me—"

"Get up, Weed."

Weed opened his gorgeous chocolatey eyes and
gazed into Mort's average-sized green ones. He noticed
they were warm and friendly. Not the eyes of an
executioner at all.

"Death will not take you today," Mort said, lifting
Weed to his feet. "Oh no, death will not take you
today."

Mort the Meek felt Mighty as he said those words.
He would definitely deserve his badge if he pulled this
off.

"I'm feeling a bit perkier," Weed said, bouncing on
the balls of his feet and shaking himself, full of energy.

"Great. This way."

"Do you have a plan?" Weed asked, jogging
alongside him.

"I do."

"Is it foolproof and failproof?"

Ah. Right. Should Mort be truthful and tell his friend that actually the plan was a bit bonkers, most probably completely stupid and might get them both beheaded in a second?

... (after all, friends never lie)

... (well?)

"Weed, it's a hundred per cent going to work."

As they made their way to the execution, people stopped and stared, and Mort wished he hadn't given Weed the Perk-me-up Potion. Weed, who really had perked up in a major way thanks to ginseng and ginger roots, was attempting that jaunty jump where you tap your feet together in the air. You know the one...

"*Look miserable,*" Mort hissed out of the side of his mouth.

"What's up with him?" a young woman asked. "Doesn't he know he's about to—" She drew a finger across her throat.

"He's gone mad," Mort said, pushing Weed on ahead.

"I'm not mad!" Weed shouted over his shoulder.

"He is!" Mort yelled.

"Not!"

They turned a corner and entered a lane thick full of the smell of milky warmth.

"This is my street!" said Weed excitedly, his nose twitching.

"Shh," Mort said. Then he added: **"Say goodbye to your family, you rotten raven-poaching worm."** (For the sake of any onlookers, of course.)

When no one was watching, Mort yanked Weed into the Millets' house, hoping they'd got everything ready.

"Mum! Dad!" Weed rushed over for hugs, but they pushed him away.

"There's no time, son," Mr Millet said. There was a job to do and time was a-ticking.

"Strip off, Weed," his mother said firmly. "Give me your clothes."

"But I don't understand—"

"Do it or else."

For some reason an 'or else' from his mum at that

moment was far more terrifying than a trip to the square for his execution, so Weed stripped. He stood in his underwear and watched in horror as his parents used his dirty clothes to dress a stark-naked child who was lying on the table. Why hadn't he noticed him? Who was this naked child being dressed in his clothes? Why didn't they give him fresh ones that weren't covered in cockroach dung? But his parents ignored his questions and Mort was too busy fiddling with a wheelbarrow to talk. Weed suddenly felt very left out of his own death-day preparations.

When they had completed their task, Mr and Mrs Millet stood back.

"Meet your replacement," Mrs Millet said, with a smile.

Weed gasped. He was being *replaced*? After he was executed, was this adopted child going to take his place as the new baker's boy?

"Meet the new baker's boy," Mr Millet said. And Weed wondered what he'd done to deserve this. "Go on, son. Say hello."

Weed tried to ignore his dad's inappropriate

happiness and approached
the child. He was going to do
something brutal as his last
act – a punch to the face or a
wrist-twist. And it wasn't until
he got nose to nose with the boy
that it hit him: that familiar scent
of freshly kneaded dough.

"He even smells like home..." Weed wailed. "He
has replaced me and I'm not even gone yet!"

"It's not real, silly boy," Weed's mum tutted.

And it wasn't. It was a Weed-sized, Weed-shaped
dough doll. The face was moulded to look like his, with
two chocolatey-coloured stones for eyes, and scruffy
brown hair, plucked from a passing dog, which had
been Semolina's idea.

"Are we ready?" Mort said tensely.

"Yes, we're ready," said a voice only Mort
recognized.

Everyone turned to look at the child with grey hair
and cloudy eyes in the doorway.

"So you got my second pigeon?" Mort said, smiling.

The child nodded.

"Who's that?" Weed asked. "And why are you talking about pigeons?"

There was no time to explain.

"Got the guts?" Mort asked the stranger.

"Got the guts," the stranger confirmed with a smile, passing Mort a small bag of fish intestines. "They absolutely stink."

Weed let out a shriek of frustration. What was going on!!!

"Weed, this is Ono Assunder, who I was telling you about."

"The talking Body Lugger? Am I going to be lugged???"

"She's going to take you to safety, and if everything goes to plan I'll see you later."

CHAPTER FIFTEEN
A BAD OMEN

"Another poor person is getting deaded, I see."

"I hope they make it quick."

"Why, so he doesn't suffer?"

"No, because I'm hungry."

While Mr and Mrs Millet hurried to join the crowds, Ono took Weed to the boat and Mort pushed the wheelbarrow through the streets to the square.

Inside it the doughy Weed doll trembled with fear (or because the Millets had used too much water in the mix) but it had the right effect, and people passing gasped at the terrible state of Weed Millet, the baker's boy. And they reeled at the terrible stench.

Mort had guts.

ABOVE BRUTALIA, THE SMELL OF DEATH PERMEATED THE FUNNY NOSTRIL HOLES AT THE TOP OF THE RAVENS' BEAKS AND THEY BEGAN TO CIRCLE...

"He used to have such warm chocolatey eyes," one woman said, shaking her head.

"I know, I know... Stone-cold they are now," said another.

"Such a pity. If I didn't love executions so much,

I'd give this one a miss."

"I know what you mean. We'd better get a wriggle on or we'll miss the carrots."

Then they hurried away, because of the carrots and the smell. The guts were ponging.

ABOVE, MORE RAVENS CIRCLED...

Mort could hear the crowd cheering – quite hoarsely now, because they'd been at it a while. The Grot Bear had been recaptured, although not without casualties. Hulk Poodle had lost a lot of his frighteningly good hair in the beast's fist during a struggle, and the Queen had gone right off him.

When Mort entered the square, the Queen stood on her balcony overlooking the stage and clapped with glee. Mort slowly rolled the wheelbarrow up the ramp and on to the stage. All eyes were on him as he lifted Weed from the wheelbarrow.

"Get up and fight, you pathetic wimp!" Mort shouted. The dough face stared back. "I said get up!"

Mort was nearly fainting from the worsening smell in his pouch.

ABOVE, EVEN MORE RAVENS CIRCLED...

Mort grabbed the dough doll by the arm, and it ripped right off.

Ooops.

"That's one I cut off earlier," Mort said, with a bold laugh.

Guards raised their *LAUGH NOW* signs and, while everyone was pretending to split their sides, Mort wiped the sweat from his brow. *That felt like a close shave!* he guessed. (He'd never actually shaved before, on account of his face being hairless.)

He wrangled the rest of his bready friend into his arms and pretended to tussle. The crowd oohed and aahed, as Mort forced a doughy arm to punch him in the eye. And the Queen screamed with glee as Mort returned the punch with a karate chop to the neck, which left a sickening dent. And then Mort, with the

162

dough doll tight in his arms, addressed the crowd.

"I am Mort the Brute and, on this day of Weed Millet's execution, I welcome you to a show of Extreme Brutality. Never before will you have witnessed such an event!"

"Sounds excellent," the Queen added. "So much better than a boring knuckle stick. Now get on with it!"

Someone in the front row of the crowd shouted, "What's that dreadful smell?"

The stink was suddenly so stinky that the air felt thick with it. The crowd began feeling ill and Mort was practically fainting.

Suddenly an almighty squawking – like a cackling soup of sound – caused everyone to look up.

RAVENS!
LOTS AND LOTS OF THEM!

They were heading for the square – a cloud of ravens so large that the sky began to turn black. The crowd screamed as if it was a really bad omen. It wasn't a bad sign for Mort, though. It meant his plan was working.

Brutalia had never seen ravens in such large numbers or heard them so aggressive. Their cries were like shattering glass, their flurry like a month of nightmares. And they were getting nearer and nearer, and nobody – nobody but Mort – knew what they wanted.

The sky inked over.

"I've got a bad feeling about this!" the Queen said. "Make the ravens go away."

WHAT?

"I said, make them go away!" she repeated. "They're scaring me! Stop the execution! I have to get out of here!"

WHAT?

"STOP IT!" she screamed. "Get that boy on his feet. I'm about to pardon him. Very quickly. Step forward, Weed Millet!" the Queen yelled. "Step forward **NOW!** I'm going to pardon you whether you like it or not."

Of course the real Weed Millet would have liked it. But the real Weed Millet was at that moment in the middle of the sea, being steered by Plop Assunder to salvation and a slap-up fruit salad down at the Landlubbers Bar. Basically there was no opportunity for a quick switcheroo, if that's what you were thinking.

Mort stopped and looked at the doughy Weed. What the curly croissants was he going to do now?

Execute 'Weed' and go against the Queen's wishes ... and **DIE?**

Or **Don't Execute 'Weed'** and reveal he just did a weird stage fight with a large piece of dough and never planned to kill Weed in the first place ... and **DIE**?

Like being faced with the choice of taking on a loving or a fighting Grot Bear – either way it was going to end badly.

"What are you doing?" yelled the Queen. "I said he's free to go."

I don't know what I'm doing, Mort thought, *because I don't have a plan called **Emergency Plan B For When Plan A Starts Going Absolutely Brilliantly**.*

There was nothing for it. He'd have to stick to Plan A. At least Weed was safe now. Mort might not be but he'd run out of choices in this brutal land.

He dropped the dough doll on to the stage floor and, as quick as a magician, he emptied his small bag of fish guts on top of it.

The billowing cloak of dark feathers, razor beaks and black button eyes dived like a great blanket of hunger on what everyone thought was Weed Millet, the baker's boy. The crowd screamed.

The gnashing, ravenous beasts feasted as if they hadn't eaten a thing in weeks, not even a rotten potato. They gnashed and screeched and gulped and ripped and clawed and tore and swallowed and, and, and...

...and within minutes there was nothing left of the baker's boy anywhere on the island of Brutalia. Not a scrap.

The birds took off as one big unkindness (which was handy as it's what you call a group of ravens, honestly). With full bellies, they went up into the sky and, when the last whisk of wing and final snap of beak had gone, no one said a word.

There was deathly silence. A silence that felt as suffocating as a woolly scarf in a summer storm.

When the shock had finally thawed, the crowd screamed louder than a screaming group of boy-band fans and a royal horn parped a **parp–pa–paaarp** ('shut up' in horn language).

Silence fell once more and all eyes turned to the Queen, who was now standing on a child for extra height, and the crowd couldn't help noticing she'd turned a strange shade of green.

"Well," the Queen said eventually, grabbing the King to steady herself and wishing she hadn't. "Explain yourself, Mort the Brute." She brought a hand to her mouth to stop herself from bringing up her oyster breakfast.

Mort stepped forward and puffed his chest out, although it was all show. His chest wasn't full of strong stuff. It was full of air – air and scare – because now he was frightened. He was really frightened, but he wasn't gutless. That was a totally different thing.

"It was my brutalist display, Your Majesty. I even named it for you. What you saw was the Ravens'

Revenge…"

(More dramatic, please.)

"THE RAVENS' REVENGE!"

(Much better!)

The Queen was not amused. "But he was pardoned!" she screamed. "I told you to stop it and you didn't! You went ahead and so… And so you have murdered an innocent child. **YOU MURDERED AN INNOCENT CHILD!"**

"I thought you said he was an adult?" Mort said nervously.

"Yes, an adult. And so I have no choice but to sentence you to **DEATH!"**

Her cry of death echoed off every wall surrounding the square, before dying away to a deathly silence. And then a voice piped up.

CHAPTER SIXTEEN
LIVE OR DIE

"Are we sticking around to see if Mort gets killed?"

"Nah, I'm stuffed."

"He's got lovely average-sized green eyeballs."

"Good point."

The voice that piped up was sneering and leering and it belonged to a man whose name spelled the same backwards.

"I think you'll find that Weed Millet **WAS** a child," Malc Clam said, stepping forward. "Inside your prison, I met Scribe Pockle, the Keeper of Birth Certificates and Legal Documents. And in my hand I have the birth certificate of Weed Millet, proving that he was in fact twelve – a whole eighteen months away from being thirteen and a half."

The crowd gasped. There were no *GASP NOW* signs but the guards were gasping too, so it didn't matter. All eyes turned once more to the Queen, who was now green from feeling a bit sick, and red from feeling a bit ashamed, or hot, or angry – it was hard to tell.

"That means, Your Majesty," Malc continued, winking at Mort who didn't have a clue what was going on, "that you sentenced a child to death. That is against the law and so..." Malc, full of purpose and righteousness and stuff, spread open his arms to address the crowd and deliver his point. "And so..."

But then the King rose to his feet and everyone looked at him instead, because he hardly ever stood up. The King opened his mouth wide. But it wasn't a belch or an oyster breakfast that came out. It was a deep baritone voice. A voice you'd expect a blue whale to have if blue whales could talk like humans. And the voice bellowed:

"OH, QUEEN, MY DARLING QUEEN. YOU'VE BEEN VERY BAD!"

"What are you talking about, you buffoon?" the Queen snapped.

"The children," the King said. "We should be protecting them."

"Why? What's got into you?"

"I like children," the King said, blushing a little. "One day I want us to have children of our own..."

"To throw to the Grot Bears?" the Queen asked.

"No! Never!" the King cried.

"Then why?"

"Because they're kind of cute."

"You never said you liked children before."

"That's because you never let me say anything, *anything*, my darling."

"But you sit on them and stand on them," the Queen spat. "You **HATE** them. We both do."

"That's not true," the King said daringly. "**YOU** have always hated them. **YOU** made me stand on them! I never wanted to."

The Queen was now flashing green, red, pink and purple, like a blinking chameleon.

Without any signs telling them how to behave, the crowd adopted crowd mentality, and all started chanting the same thing:

"OFF WITH HER HEAD! OFF WITH HER HEAD! OFF WITH HER HEAD!"

The Queen's guards didn't know what to do.

"OFF WITH HER HEAD! OFF WITH HER HEAD! OFF WITH HER HEAD!"

The roar got louder and louder. The crowd stamped their feet. They were no longer worried about the ravens or a boy named Weed. They were united as one, and calling for Mort to kill the Queen.

"Go on, Mort. Kill the Queen!" shouted one, to make sure that was understood.

Then things sped up a bit. The indecisive guards got decisive all of a sudden. They circled the Queen and marched her down to the stage, and the King started to flap his hands in confusion. He loved his wife to the moon and back, but at the same time he had to admit she was a bit of a stinker and probably deserved the knuckliest of all knuckle sticks for the terrible things she'd done. But she was his first love, his only love, and everyone should get a second chance, shouldn't they...? He rammed his fist in his mouth to stop himself from blubbing.

Mort the Brute looked down. The tiny hazel-gazey eyes of the Queen of Brutalia locked with his average-sized green ones.

This mean-lipped, mean-eyed, cruel ruler with a long history of punishing people for choosing to live deserved to die. But Mort knew the Pacifist Promise he made every day. He'd made it that very morning.

I, a member of the Pacifist Society of Brutalia, promise not to hurt anything.

I promise not to hurt anything. I promise not to hurt anything.

The Queen was definitely a thing.

Thinking her hazel-gazey eyes hadn't worked their magic, the Queen twisted her face into an almighty scrunch.

"I knew I shouldn't have made you Royal Executioner," she spat. And then she spat. She really was a horrible woman.

Within a minute, Mort could have the Queen's head right off and then Brutalia would be free from her vile behaviour and free from executions. And then perhaps it could become like Dead Man's Island, a place of peace and happiness and kindness and fruit salads. If only he wasn't a fully signed-up member of the Pacifist Society of Brutalia... If only.

Wait a minute. Let's go back again.

Free from executions...
Free from executions...
Free from executions...
Free from executions...

Free from executions...

Free from executions...

"Heavens!" Mort gasped. Just by thinking of that bounteous island, he had allowed his mind to soar way above the rickety crossed towers – it gave him a new perspective and an excellent idea.

A marvellous idea.

A stupendous idea.

A fantabilissimissimus idea.

(Get on with it!)

Right. Sorry. We're all just very excited about this idea.

Even better, this time Mort's idea came all at once and not bit by bit, saving some precious time.

Mort beckoned to Malc Clam, who brought him parchment and paper, and for Scribe Pockle, who brought the royal stamp. Mort scribbled furiously, a grin spreading across his face as he realized pacifist history was being made right here, in the brutal land of Brutalia, by the Pacifist Society of Brutalia. And its only member.

When he was finished, Mort held his arms in the air to ask for silence.

"Do you want me to execute the Queen?" he called.

"YES, YES, GET ON WITH IT ALREADY!" came the shout from the crowd.

"Well then," Mort said, looking at the Queen. "The time has come."

The Queen had now lost her mean demeanour (which is full of mean in so many ways). Her hard, pinched face had fallen into broad despair, her hazel-gazey eyes were swimming in salty water and her bottom lip was all aquiver...

"Stand up, Queenie," Mort ordered.

The Queen rose to her feet on trembling legs.

Mort banged his knuckle stick and a giant

$SHUSH$ ran round the square.

And, when it had finished running, it stopped altogether and vanished and then there was nothing but the whistle of the wind and the sound of an evil Queen sobbing.

Realizing he was behaving a little like his uncle but going with it, Mort waited until all eyes were on him. Then he stepped forward, arms stretched wide. But he didn't say what anyone expected him to say. Rather extraordinarily he said, "I can bring back Weed Millet."

$WHAT?$ (everyone thought).

"You what?" the Queen said.

"I said, I can bring back Weed Millet."

"Are you a witch?" the Queen said, hazel eyes not gazey, but narrowing with suspicion.

"Are you about to have your head chopped off?" Mort snapped, reminding her that she wasn't in a position to be judgemental.

"*Hmngnnng,*" the Queen growled. "Go on."

"Your Majesty, if I bring back Weed Millet, it will mean that he is not dead and you are not guilty of sentencing a child to death. So shall I or shall I not?"

"Yes, please!" the Queen said, grabbing Mort's legs and pleading like a dog that wants biscuits.

"On one condition," Mort said. "You sign the bottom of this document. With Scribe Pockle's stamp, it will be binding, and if you do break the rules written within then you will be back here on this stage, facing death once again. Do you understand?"

The Queen rolled her eyes.

"Queenie..." Mort warned.

"Oh, all right."

Without further ado, she signed her name on a document that bound her to follow the rules that Mort had laid out.

"Darling, you're going to live!" the King boomed, before he fainted with relief and fell, squashing three small children.

Mort took the parchment and read it out to the Queen and the crowd.

"**RULE 1**: If I bring back Weed, there shall be NO questions asked."

"What do you mean there shall be no questions asked?" the Queen quizzed, wrinkling her nose.

"That's a question," Mort said.

Someone in the crowd called, "Off with her head!"

"Don't ask any more questions," Mort advised her.

"**RULE 2**: From this day forward, our motto of LIVE OR DIE shall be changed to LIVE AND LET LIVE."

People clapped and they also shrugged because they didn't really understand what that meant. In time they would learn. But 'in time' is very vague – it could mean minutes or centuries, which we certainly don't have time for, so let's move on.

"**RULE 3**: There shall be no more violent non-death punishments."

"**RULE 4**: There shall be no more executions in Brutalia."

Stunned silence.

Mort said it louder.

"No more executions."

That did it. The crowd erupted in cheers and whoops and they danced with linked arms. Hats and cabbages and pigeons were thrown in the air, as was customary. It took everyone a mighty long time to calm down, because in all the excitement toes were trodden on. That led to punches being thrown, noses being tweaked and shins being kicked. But, all in all, everybody looked very happy indeed.

Almost everybody.

"What about the free carrots?"

The croaky voice belonged to an old crone called Sally McRoot, who made her living selling carrot soup.

"*What about the free carrots?*" she asked again.

Mort grabbed the quill from Malc Clam and quickly scrawled on the document.

"**RULE 5**: Free carrots will be thrown every Saturday."

"Thanks," said Sally McRoot, with a nod of the head.

Mort turned back to the terrifically jubilant crowd

and it was hard to tell what they were more delighted about – the end of executions or the guaranteed free carrots. But it mattered not, because he had made pacifist history here on the cruel rock of Brutalia.

He banged the knuckle stick again, for no other reason than he quite liked the attention. He then had to quickly think of something else to say. Something stirring and final and brilliant and chapter-ending.

"The document has been signed by Her Royal Majesty, the Queen of Brutalia, and is now legally binding. People of Brutalia, you are free to live as you please. Be good people, be kind and be happy. From this day onwards, you no longer have to fear for your lives."

CHAPTER SEVENTEEN
FAREWELLS

(Er ... where are the ravens?)

Mort and Ono stood side by side on the spiky shore of Brutalia while Weed tried to find his land legs. (*If you spend a long time on a boat, you grow sea legs, which can only run sideways.*)

"Weed is safe and Brutalia is free. Why don't you come back with me?" Ono said. "You deserve a holiday."

Mort looked deep into Ono's cloudy-coloured eyes, which were like portals into that pacifists' paradise. He could see himself down at the Landlubbers Bar, making jokes with sailors and playing in the surf, picking exotic fruits and growing marigolds... How he would love that!

But what about Gosh and Gee and the promises he made to them as they lay in their beds with turnip slices on their heads? And what about his parents' ongoing feud with the next-door neighbours? He needed to do something before someone got forked. And what if he, the only pacifist living in Brutalia, left? Then there would be no one to spread the word of peace...

"There are things I need to do here, Ono."

She looked at him with deep and meaningful eyes. She blinked.

"OK, no worries," she said. "Come and see me some day."

It looked as if Weed's legs had started walking straight... Nope, he veered off into the side of the cliff again.

"Wait, Ono," Mort said, taking her hand. "The look in your eyes was so deep and meaningful. What were they saying?"

"Goodbye."

Without another word, Ono ran across the shattered shore and climbed aboard her father's boat. Silently, swiftly, they pushed the boat off. A big wave swelled up in front of them and Mort lost sight of her. When the wave subsided, she was already far away.

"Bye-bye, Mort the Brute," she called, her voice faint on the wind.

"I'm not *Mort the Brute!*" he shouted.

"I know. I was being sarcastic, you plonker."

Mort suddenly thought of something and he waved like crazy.

"Actually, I'm Mort the Mighty!" he shouted into the gusts.

But there was nothing to see but the fretting sea. Ono was gone.

Weed stood next to Mort, holding on to his shoulder for support and wobbling only slightly.

"Where's Ono?"

"Gone, Weed. Gone."

"Did she say anything deep and meaningful before she left?"

"Not really."

"Did she say anything about me?"

"Yes," Mort said. "She said it was, er, lovely to meet you." It was a lie but Mort got the feeling it would mean a lot to Weed, and it wasn't hurting anyone. Not hurting anyone was his speciality.

"What else did she say? Did she say I was special? Did she say anything about my good looks and big chocolatey eyes?"

Mort looked into those chocolate eyes, so hopeful...

But lying twice was probably a bit much.

"She might have been thinking it," Mort said, "but she didn't say it. I have a feeling there was a lot she didn't say."

But Mort said that bit to himself, because Weed's legs had wheeled him round in a semicircle back towards the sea.

"Stop!" Mort shouted, fearful that the vicious drag of the ocean would pull his friend in. Which it did.

After a wet struggle with the waves, which left them with urchin-spiked feet and seaweed down their pants, Mort and Weed flopped on to the pitiless beach, panting and gasping.

"One day you're going to get bored of saving me," Weed said. "You are, you know."

Mort raised himself on his elbows and a thought struck him harder than a conch shell on the bonce.

"No. I would never get bored of saving you. Don't you see, Weed? Saving you is what saved me. It's what saved Brutalia!"

"Urgh! Is that a crab on my toe?"

Mort ignored Weed's marine-based troubles as his

mind tumbled and turned over the events of the last few days.

"Our friendship changed everything, Weed. When both of us were faced with the worst fate possible, neither of us had anything to lose – and that meant we had everything to fight for. No one ever tried to change Brutalia's rules before, but we did. And it worked! It didn't have to be **LIVE OR DIE** at all. The Queen's motto was a lie. We can make other choices. Nothing is that black and white…"

An image of Ono nodding and giving him a thumbs up appeared in his mind.

"Do you think that was deep and meaningful enough for a final scene?" Mort raised his eyebrows in question.

"Absolutely. That was **SO** deep and meaningful," Weed said, his warm chocolatey eyes swimming with admiration. "Can we go now?"

"Yeah, all right."

Mort and Weed ran back up the rocks and through the foul-smelling backstreets and piddling side streets of Brutalia. But they were stopped in their tracks by this:

ARRRGHHHHHHH!

What was that?

There was screaming from the square... Not from one person, but lots and lots of persons. It was worse than the yelling at a vegetable fight or the shriek of someone being forced to pull the Queen's chariot with their earlobes, more desperate than the runaway screams of anyone close to the King's bottom...

It was the sound of great, great terror.

Brutalia had heard that sound only once before... Just the day before, as it happens.

"What on earth is that?" Mort said, looking at Weed anxiously.

"It sounds like hell," Weed said. He started to shake. "Mort, did we just break Brutalia?"

"I don't know. Let's find out."

The boys ran round the corner, where black birds were plummeting from the sky like cannonballs, dive-bombing the terrified people below. There was mass panic in the square – people, ravens, arms, legs, wings, carrots – and an almighty screeching, like the sound of tortured demons. It was a rain of terror.

"What have you done to the ravens?" Weed yelled. "You've turned them into man-eating monsters! It's the ... RAVENS' REVENGE!"

(More dramatic, please.)

THE RAVENS' REVENGE!

(Much better!)

It certainly looked a bit revenge-y.

Mort froze as he gazed in horror at the doom he had created.

But staying still and not running around meant he could see between everyone's legs and he could hear between their screams. And the noise he heard was:

Weeeeee–plop–boing

"Shh," Mort said. "Did you hear that?"

"What, the sound of imminent death?" Weed shouted, wide-eyed.

Weeeeee–plop–boing

Mort began laughing.

"WHAT IS IT?" Weed insisted.

Mort pointed up at the dive-bombing ravens.

Weeeeee–plop–boing

"That, my friend, is not the sound of imminent death. It's the sound of a raven that has eaten too much uncooked dough and has fallen out of the sky, bounced a bit, and is now rolling on the ground with its legs in the air."

"Oi! What are they laughing at?"

People had started to notice the two boys chuckling happily as if death wasn't imminent. And, as no one had actually died yet, they calmed down a bit and became curious as to why. Looking around, they soon saw what Mort and Weed had seen – startled ravens, not resembling the winged, foul-stinking breath of a giant bird devil ... but bloated, feathery balls.

It started as a ripple, then a wave, and then a whole sea of laugher washed over the square. People were doubled over in hysterics – this divine comedy was something they'd never witnessed. And it was delightful!

But then the Brutalia instinct returned. And between the shouts of, *That's the funniest thing I've seen since Uncle Kevin fell off the roof*, and eruptions

of laughter so intense that wobbly teeth flew out, there
were shouts of:

"Bird ball!"

"Yeah, bird ball!"

"Kick the bird balls!"

"Kick them really hard!"

Kids of all ages began running at the ravens.

Oh no! That's not very pacifist-y!

Mort grabbed a guard's horn that lay abandoned
from the kerfuffle of the day before and put it to his lips.

Pa-Pa-PAAAAAAAARP!

Everyone stopped, because it had become a habit
to stop when a royal horn parped. They turned to see
Mort clambering on top of the stage where so much
had happened. He stretched out his arms to the people
imploringly.

"Do not hurt the ravens!" he called. "It's the ravens
that helped bring about the end of Brutalia's reign of
death and pain and cruelty."

"Oh yeah," said lots of people.

"Think about it," Mort continued. "It was the capture of a hungry raven that began this sorry story and the feeding of ravens that freed us."

Mort hoped that would be enough because he couldn't think of how else the ravens helped, but luckily everyone agreed that the ravens were pretty special. Apart from Punky Mason, the daughter of a rock-crusher, who had a very bad attitude.

"But I want to kick something!" she snarled loudly.

"And you *can* kick something. We can all kick things," Mort said. "But we'll find round objects that don't have feelings. Is that OK?"

Punky Mason nodded. "Y'all right."

"What's more, we'll form a sports team, and the ravens will be our round-object-kicking emblem. We shall call our team the Brutalia Ravens!"

(Feel free to draw a raven emblem here.)

There was a pleasing roar, as big as one you'd hear at a professional round-object-kicking stadium. And people began to pick up the swollen-bellied ravens and stroke them tenderly. They were going to take them home, name them and nurse them back to the glossy-coated and handsome birdy beasts they once were.

Apart from Sally McRoot, whom Mort heard muttering something about a raven-and-carrot surprise. He sighed and shook his head. He couldn't change Brutalia's habits overnight but he would work on it.

He'd dedicate his life to working on it.

He'd work on it daily and nightly.

Most of all, he'd work on it Mightily.

"I've got a feeling that things are going to be different from now on," Weed said. "Maybe you can teach me to be a pacifist. What do you say?" Weed punched Mort's arm affectionately but very hard.

"First lesson tomorrow," Mort said, rubbing his throbbing arm.

"See ya, Mort," Weed said. Then he scooped up a fat raven, named him Mister Munchy and waved goodbye.

Mort took another look round the square. Where once there was a sense of dread, there was now an air of promise – the promise of a peaceful future.

He smiled as he walked back home through the less-sinister side streets and not-so-abysmal backstreets of Brutalia. He knew that his mum and dad would be ding-donging with the neighbours, and those ratbag-muffins, Gosh and Gee, would immediately kick him in the kneecaps and smash him over the head with a frying pan. But he was looking forward to it.

And he was looking forward to sewing a very special badge on his pyjamas, just as soon as he got the design right.

THE END

(Please use this space to design a Mort the Mighty
badge because he's having trouble with it.)

JOIN MORT ON HIS NEXT ADVENTURE IN...

MORT THE MEEK

THE MONSTROUS QUEST

RACHEL DELAHAYE

ILLUSTRATED BY GEORGE ERMOS

DEAR UNFORTUNATE
READERS — A WARNING

This is not your average tale. This is not a jolly page-turner before bedtime. Oh no – it's definitely not that. This is a story that swims through a world of weirdness without armbands, and not everyone has the stomach, eyes and teeth for such a thing. If you don't have the stomach, eyes and teeth for such a thing, then leave now.

Are you still here?

All right, let's try again...

DEAR UNFORTUNATE READERS WHO HAVE THE STOMACH, EYES AND TEETH FOR SUCH A THING...

This tale contains no fewer than FOUR trips to sea, a barrage of SLIMY insults and some seriously TORMENTED characters. If you get seasick, or if you're nice, or if you'd rather not discover the dark side of human nature, I advise you to leave now.

Are you still here?

Then you're mad. Mad as a kipper's slippers. And you'll probably enjoy this horrible story. Read on, but let's start at the real Chapter One.

THE REAL CHAPTER ONE
THERE WERE SIGNS

There were signs. Signs were there. Were there signs...?

(This chapter is called THERE WERE SIGNS, so yes, there probably were.)

In fact, there were LOADS of signs. They were on every wall, pillar and roof. On every raven that stood still long enough for someone to stick a piece of paper on (and there were quite a few). Brutalia was covered and they all said:

Citizens of Beautiful Brutalia,
Gather in the square tonight for some news.
Your Divine Queen

Well! The citizens of Beautiful Brutalia fell backwards in shock for two reasons:

1.   The signs were scented – they wafted sweet smells as they flapped in the wind (or on ravens) and people had never sniffed 'sweet' before. The island reeked of rot. And the only perfume available was Eau de Errr, sold by perfumer Olfa Smelch in buckets (although he called them boutiques) called Olfa Smelch Smells (and he really did).

2.   The Queen's orders were normally belched door to door by one of the Queen's guards, not written down. But weirder than that was the word BEAUTIFUL. People rolled the strange word round in their mouths until it got all spitty, and they were as baffled as bath plugs on the moon.

You see, it's hard to explain beautiful to those who have only ever known grime, grunge and grot, and lots of other horrid things beginning with 'g'. Because life on Brutalia could never be beautiful. Have you been there? If you have, I'm surprised you're not missing three toes and an earlobe. If you haven't been there before, then hold on to your churning guts because WELCOME TO BAD LUCK, YOU'RE IN BRUTALIA.

Brutalia was a spiky island in the Salty Sea that attracted precisely no one. Its reputation was cruel, its jagged coastline skewered sailors quicker than a kebab and there was a rotten stink that clung to it like mist on a bog. The rotten stink was actually a cloud of despair (a key ingredient of Eau de Errr). And despair was always there – in the air, in your hair, under there, everywhere. No sailor with a brain or a nose would stop for the night. Not unless they wanted a visit to hell.

Because that's what Brutalia was: hellish.

Beneath the island's raven-infested watchtowers, in a single city brimming with filth, Brutalians fought. They fought for food; they fought to survive; they fought to feel alive. Even Brutalia's littlest kids lived for a punch-up. They roamed the streets in gangs, offering tooth removal, using the traditional method of Fist-to-Face.

Who could possibly let them live like this! I hear you cry.

I'll tell you who – the Queen and King of Brutalia. And they were royally revolting.

The King was a bit smelly, but it was the Queen who was the real stinker. She had the compassion of a brick. She loved no one and cared for nothing – and if she had known about the King's secret pet cockroach, Corky, she'd have killed him without batting her stick-on beetle-leg eyelashes. That's the kind of person she was.

So you see, explaining the word beautiful to a Brutalian was like trying to describe a new colour or a new taste. But there it was, on all those signs: Beautiful.

Sweet smells, pretty signs, strange words... Something fishy was going on. Was it good fishy or bad fishy? The people would have to go to the square to find out. And they would also have to go to the square because that's what the Queen had ordered. If they didn't, they'd end up getting Punishment of the Day.

But we're getting sidetracked now, and you don't want to get sidetracked in Brutalia or you might end up down a dark alley getting your teeth knocked out by a bunch of rascals.

(Told you there was nothing nice about this place.)

CHAPTER TWO
GOD, REALLY?

The square was packed and the royal procession out
in full, complete with cooks, servants and royal pets.
These were official pets, such as manky-breath tigers
and giant lizards on leads (and definitely not Corky,
the King's secret cockroach). The Queen had even
brought out her Grot Bears, which usually made an
entrance only on sports days. They were grotesque,
bear-like creatures with small brains and big paws
and they were present for one reason: to make the
crowd behave. If these beasts were let loose, there'd
be all sorts of trouble. Depending on what sort of Grot
Bear got hold of you – a loving one or a fighting one –
you'd either be bear-hugged and crushed to death or
ripped apart.

Guards held up *QUIET NOW* signs, although
at the sight of the Grot Bears an uneasy silence had
already fallen over the square. There was no noise

apart from the revolting slurp of Grot Bears trying to lick their own eyeballs, and the occasional growl of a manky-breath tiger.

On a high stage in the middle of the square, the Queen was helped up on to her long-legged chair, the seat of which was up a ladder and padded with ten cushions.

"Behold your God!" she said.

Being so high up, her voice was faint and no one heard a thing. Not even the guards below, who were too far away to kick. She plucked a megaphone from her skirts and tried again.

"Behold your God!" she shouted and raised her arms to the sky.

Confused, everyone looked up, spotted a seagull and guessed they should play along. "We worship you, o seagull," they mumbled.

"ME, you imbeciles. ME!" the Queen shrieked. The seagull plopped something sticky on her shoulder and the air was thick with awkwardness.

The guards quickly held up signs that said *CHEER NOW*. The people did as they were told and hurrahed enthusiastically. Everyone apart from Mort Canal, the plumber's son. With his father, brother and sister missing at sea, he couldn't have produced a hooray even if he'd wanted to. Not even a little one.

"Try!" urged Weed Millet, the baker's son, who was Mort's best friend.

"Hu-urgh…"

"That's not a cheer – that's a ticket straight to the dungeons. Quick, get behind me."

The Queen no longer carried out executions, but she was still hugely keen on locking people in small dark spaces infested with rats, and she always sent spies into the crowd to root out disobedient subjects. Weed stood in front of Mort to hide him and cheered extra loudly for both of them.

Despite the huge chorus of forced cheers, the Queen began waving her arms and shouting, "Come on! Praise me, you despicable worms!"

"She's totally off her rocker!" Mort whispered.

Weed turned and nodded. "Totally barking," he mouthed back, before Weed's beady-eyed mother shoved dough balls in their mouths. Whispering, mouthing, sometimes even breathing – the Queen could make anything punishable by Punishment of the Day if she felt like it. And the punishment was clearly written on a chalkboard in the square.

PUNISHMENT OF THE DAY

HORNET PANTS

Scream in agony as you are lowered into underwear
lined with the Queen's royal hornets
Please note: screaming is punishable by...

JELLYFISH PANTS

Scream in agony as you are lowered into underwear
lined with the Queen's royal jellyfish
Please note: screaming is punishable by...

CACTUS PANTS

Scream in agony as you are lowered into underwear
lined with the Queen's royal cactus...
(You get the picture.)

"Yes, my loyal subjects, it's true. An old document found in the palace vaults has revealed that I am not mortal, like the rest of you snivelling losers. I am, in fact, descended from GODS. Actual GODS!"

The guards raised CLAP NOW signs and everyone obeyed, of course. The Queen smiled languidly, waiting for the clapping to die down. It took a while – no one wanted to be the first to stop; no one wanted to try on those hornet pants for size. When she'd had enough glory and was certain that every citizen's hands were red raw with effort, she beckoned to the guards to lower the signs.

ACKNOWLEDGEMENTS

Firstly, an enormous thank-you to my agent, Alice Williams, who, with the patience of a saint, has helped me become a better writer. And to my 24/7 cheerleaders – Dandy Smith, David Gamlin, Sophie Gamlin, Vanessa Ferret, Katie Preedy, Victoria Walker and Lucy Wendover – who read my words and support me in so much. And to Susie Chadwick and Sarah Wratten, who are always there. What wonderful friends you are.

Eternal thanks to Mike, Matilda and Ben for giving me love and food and the essential time and space to write. I am stupidly lucky to have the inexhaustible support of my biggest fan – my mum (who reads, critiques and tells me my spelling is terrible). Without her wit, wisdom and red pen, I'd be nothing.

Thanks to librarian extraordinaire Nicki Cleveland and her eager readers who first tested this book many moons ago, and big love to my band of Twitter friends in the book community for their friendship and encouragement, which helps more than they know.

Of course, gargantuan cheers must be whooped for my talented illustrator, George Ermos, who has made Mort glorious.

And last but not least, I'd like to express my deep gratitude to everyone at Little Tiger – to the editorial and marketing teams, to Thy, Marg and Kimberley for design, and to my smashing editor, Mattie Whitehead: Mattie, thank you for falling in love with Mort and making all this happen.

Rachel Delahaye was born in Australia but
has lived in the UK since she was six years old.
She studied linguistics and worked as a magazine
writer and editor before becoming a children's author.
Rachel loves reading, cooking and wandering about
in woodlands. Somewhere in between all that she
writes. She especially enjoys writing comedy and says,
profoundly: Life without comedy is like cereal without
milk – dry and hard to swallow.

Rachel has two lively children and a dog called Rocket,
and lives in the beautiful city of Bath.

George Ermos is an illustrator, maker and avid
reader from England. He works digitally and enjoys
illustrating all things curious and mysterious.